Annie Thomas

No Hero, but a Man

A Novel: Vol.III.

Annie Thomas

No Hero, but a Man
A Novel: Vol.III.

ISBN/EAN: 9783337067557

Printed in Europe, USA, Canada, Australia, Japan

Cover: Foto ©Andreas Hilbeck / pixelio.de

More available books at **www.hansebooks.com**

NO HERO, BUT A MAN.

NO HERO,
BUT A MAN.

A Novel.

BY

ANNIE THOMAS

(*Mrs Pender-Cudlip*),

AUTHOR OF
'DENIS DONNE,' 'THE HONOURABLE JANE,' 'A GIRL'S FOLLY,'
'UTTERLY MISTAKEN,' ETC., ETC.

IN THREE VOLUMES.

VOL. III.

LONDON:

F. V. WHITE & CO.,
14 BEDFORD STREET, STRAND, W.C.

1894

CONTENTS.

---o---

CHAPTER I.

CHAPTER VII.

CHAPTER VIII.

CHAPTER IX.

CHAPTER X.

CHAPTER XI.

NO HERO, BUT A MAN.

NO HERO, BUT A MAN.

CHAPTER I.

HIS GOOD INFLUENCE—FAILS!

'HE has swallowed the bait! I have him on my hook, and can play him as I please,' Mrs Gaston thought triumphantly when 'Mr Harlby' was announced by the maid who condescended to answer the front-door bell while her mistress was in lodgings.

Their last interview had been one of suppressed storm, and (on her side) insulting satire. But these facts, though she remembered them clearly enough, exercised neither a subduing nor an embarrassing influence over her now. Nothing, indeed, with the exception of *mal de mer*, had ever subdued or embarrassed her since her marriage with a man who had made his pile. She would have laughed the idea to scorn had anyone suggested that anything besides poverty and a bad head could possibly depress her.

'Oh! come ye in peace here, or come ye in war?' she quoted merrily, as she turned from the open window through which she had been looking at the sea, and wishing that she could step into her New York mansion

without the painful preliminary of passing at least five or six days on the
ocean's treacherous surface. She held
her hand out to him as she spoke,
and with her back to the light, which
was tempered by rose silk curtains,
she looked very well in her beautifully
cut gown and cool assurance.

'In peace! I shouldn't have come
otherwise,' he said quietly. He had
touched her hand courteously, but
without warmth or cordiality, and his
face was as stern as if he were founded
on a social rock, and had her at his
mercy instead of the reverse being the
case, as she wished him to believe.

He had given one hasty glance
round the room when he entered, and
she read disappointment in his face
when he saw that she was its sole

occupant.   Answering   his   unspoken
thought   instead   of   his   words,   she
said,—

'I have not brought you here on
a fool's errand. Miss Woodford will
be here directly. I sent her out into
the village in order that I might see
you alone for a few minutes if you
came, as I felt sure you would come
this morning. Let me caution you,
she doesn't know I wrote to you. Let
her think you have come of your
own free will.'

'I never have, and never will, deceive her,' he said, and the hot blood
rushed into his face as he spoke.

'No, I am surprised,' she said, with
pretended archness and genuine malice.

'Why surprised?'

'Oh, I mean nothing, I assure you,

more than this, that men invariably do deceive women, especially the women they are in love with.'

'I am an exception to your rule,' he said shortly.

'And *she* is the exception to *your* rule, I suppose ?'

'You speak in riddles, Mrs Gaston.'

'Then I will speak more plainly in all friendly openness. Can you look me in the face and tell me that you have not deceived a great number of people since my old friend Herbert Harlby died so suddenly ?'

'You must speak more plainly.'

'No, there is no occasion for me to do so. You can fill in the blanks I leave. Remember, I was able to tell you of the existence of a secret receptacle in the black bag you claimed as your own.'

'And I am able to tell you what was in it,' he said quietly.

'Impossible!'

'But true, nevertheless. It contained the photograph of a lady, and some fearlessly free outpourings of feminine affection. I was not interested either in the preservation or destruction of these articles, therefore I let them remain in their hiding-place. If you had asked me for them I would have given them to you, and spared you the trouble of bribing one of my servants to commit the dishonest act of taking the bag without leave. I don't call it by such a harsh name as " stealing."'

For a few moments she looked at

him irresolutely. Then, with rather a
strained laugh, she said,—

'So you feel you can afford to
defy me, even if I were to turn as
malicious as most women would under
the circumstances.'

'I don't defy you, Mrs Gaston. I
shall only continue to act without regard to you in any way.'

'In fact, you feel—or fancy—that I
have no power to cast suspicion on
you, or your claims.'

'The consideration of you or your
possible course of action does not
weigh with me one way or the other.'

'Then the widow of the man by
whose death you have gained temporary possession of Gunwalloe must be
in collusion with you to wrong her
own son !'

'I came here in peace, but that will not be maintained long if you speak disparagingly of Mrs Harlby. I came here also on the strength of your representations of good - will and friendly feeling towards Miss Woodford with regard to myself. You appear to have forgotten them.'

'Why should I trouble myself to make crooked matters straight between you and Miss Woodford, when you are ready to tilt at any windmill on account of Mrs Harlby? You can't be in real earnest about Miss Woodford, and, as her friend, I must tell her so frankly, while you go round proclaiming your readiness to do knight-errant's work for the widow.'

'Your ideas of chivalry or knight-errantry are—excuse me,—more than rather limited!'

'So are the ideas of most nine-teenth-century men on that same sub-ject,' she answered promptly. Then with a quick change of manner she added,—

'Pardon me! I only spoke according to my lights. I hear Miss Woodford coming in. I say peace! and I will stand your friend with her.'

She passed him and met Frances at the door just in time to gently push the latter back into the tiny passage and whisper,—

'Be very kind to him. You are his good influence. That other woman will drag him down in spite of himself if *you* don't intervene to bring out what is best in him.'

Frances was only human, and pure womanly into the bargain. She kindled (against her judgment) to the idea of bringing out what was 'best' in the man she loved, who had twice asked her to marry him, and of intervening beneficially for him between Rose Harlby and his 'worst impulses.' Naturally Frances thought that only inferior, not to say *bad*, impulses, could direct him towards any other woman than herself. So with all the spirit of a rescuer filling her soul, she went in to meet him in the little rose-light softened room in which he looked large, manly, strong and '*real!*' she felt in spite of everything!

'I *am* surprised,' she said, with much more more pleasure than surprise in her tone.

'Will you tell me I am welcome, Frances?'

'You know that I can't help being glad to see you, Mr Harlby! It is not quite fair of you to surprise me into admitting it, though. I have been thinking of you enjoying yourself at Gunwalloe and on board the *White Heather*. Youth at the helm, and Pleasure at the prow, the centre of a circle of admiring friends, all ready to extol *Mr Harlby*, and applaud everything he does. It strikes me as odd rather, therefore, that you should come to me who neither extol you nor applaud what you are doing.'

'You know how to make words sting! but, you love me.'

'Don't taunt me with my miserable weakness. I do love you, God help me; but what does my love bring me but a constant gnawing dread, a perpetual nervous pain? You know why I feel these things on your account, yet you go on living the life that causes me anguish, and at the same time descend to the mean depths of reminding me that my heart is traitor to my mind and reason in *loving* you.'

'The life I am leading? What is there in the life I am leading to cause you displeasure — much more "anguish"?'

'How can you ask? when you know—'

'What?'

'What I know! If you would only tell me that it was the madness of a moment, that you are repentant and remorseful, and ready to give up *every-*

thing — everything — and bear whatever the penalty of the fraud may be—'

' Fraud ! We are getting out of our depths, indeed, when you can use such a word about a man you say you *love !* '

' Will you give up Gunwalloe, the position, the friends, and the esteem you have gained. Will you stand confessed openly as what you are ? If you will, I am ready to openly avow my love for you, and share your fortunes, however poor they may be.'

' My own darling ! bless you for your love and brave words. But I already stand openly confessed as what I am. Nothing can undo the facts that I was born a Harlby and christened Herbert.'

' And nothing can undo the fact that

you knew nothing of Gunwalloe until
the other Herbert Harlby's sudden death
put you in possession of his effects, and
enabled you to establish your heirship.
Oh! what a miserable woman I am to
be the only one who fully understands
your guilt, and, at the same time, the
only one who fully loves you.'

'My guilt! my guilt!' he repeated,
questioningly. 'Ah! I see! You think,
as I did in the first Quixotic burst
of feeling, when I found he had left a
widow and son, that I ought to have
effaced myself for their benefit. Some-
times I feel that still; but Rose would
never accept the sacrifice, and moreover, it would revive and rip open an
ugly family story. You may believe
me or not, Frances, but I swear to
you, as a man of honour, that the

hand I offer you again is an unsoiled one.'

' I would give half the remaining years of my life to believe you,' she said deliberately ; ' but, if I pretended to do so, my conscience would be pandering to my love ' Then the re-collection of his having spoken of the pretty young widow as ' Rose,' smote her like a stinging - nettle, and she added,—

' " Rose," as you call her, must prize you above her child, if she would not accept the " sacrifice " of seeing you cede his rights to him. After all, per-haps, I *ought* to hope that her devotion to you and your interests will smooth the way to an arrangement that will leave poor baby Gerald in possession of some of his rights eventually.'

'You think me cur enough to have defrauded him of them?'

'I think — oh! what *do* I think! I only know that I am the most wretched of women! You look so noble — so proud—so manly! and I, wretched, weak fool that I am, can't separate you from your personality. I love you for what you look to be! I despise you for what I know you are. And all the time it is your personality — my ideal — which sways me, and not the poor, faulty, fallen bit of humanity you are.'

'And all this because I am not willing to proclaim myself an impostor, and give up my birthright?'

'All this because you are not man enough to stand forward and say I was tempted, I was weak, I fell.'

'I *was* weak, and no mistake, but not in the way you think.'

'Why, oh! why didn't I *die* before you crossed my path again, after that fearful day in the railway carriage.'

'Because you were destined to live to love me,' he said with a sudden change from the manner of accused to accuser, 'destined to be loved by me, and, unless you soften, to break my heart.'

'Unless I *lower*, you mean?'

'You can't take me on trust, then? You refuse to be guided by instinct and feeling?'

'I do. Thank God my reason is unimpaired. I am foolishly, but not madly, fond of you.'

'It would not satisfy you if I made a quiet surrender of all you have enumerated, Gunwalloe, position, friends, good repute, everything in fact that I value, besides yourself?'

She shook her head, and put on a look of stern sweetness that bound her fetters faster round her.

'There would be no atonement in a quiet surrender, that left you un-blemished, and so unpunished, in the eyes of the world. I want your ex-piation to be as open as your fault was great. In surrendering all you value in addition to myself *quietly*, *secretly*, you would have to surrender me too.'

'Do you mean that if the whole world looked askance at me as a found-out fool, you would acknow-ledge me still?'

'If the whole world scouted you

for making open restitution, I would stand as closely as you liked by your side, and I should be prouder of you than—than any of your summer friends are now—whatever their professions may be.'

'The thing you tempt me to do is impossible. I burnt my boats behind me when I claimed my own, when that poor fellow died.'

'Was he not the rightful heir? Oh, Herbert, I would give up the thing that is dearest to me in the world, to have you look me straight in the eyes, and say, "He was the impostor, not I."'

'He was not an utter impostor. What he assumed, and what he did, he assumed in partial ignorance.'

'Then if he was not an impostor,

or shall I say a fraudulent pretender?
What are you?'

'A most unhappy man in not being
able to dispel doubts in your mind
which wrong me.'

'Is that all you will tell me? You
are selfish.'

'Good heavens, if I thought only of
myself, I should make a clean breast
of everything to you and the world at
once. But I am held back by consideration for the honour of the dead
and the happiness of the living.'

'You have been more than cruel in
seeking me again, Mr Harlby. I was
not happy, but, at least, I was at super-
ficial peace until I saw you again to-
day. Now I feel as if I could never
know rest again.'

He had been looking away, frown-

ingly, over the sea as she spoke,
unable (so it seemed to her) to meet
her direct gaze. As her last words
faltered out, with such an obvious strain-
ing after moderate composure that they
betrayed her misery more absolutely than
any burst of emotion would have done,
he turned round, but he was too late.
The door was closing behind her. She
was gone, and with her the chance of
freeing himself from his Quixotic fetters,
in her eyes at least, was gone also.

'Have you been kind and sensible?'
Mrs Gaston asked, as Frances ran
against her on the stairs, where she
had been standing, not 'listening,' but
still hearing a good deal of what had
transpired between her companion and
Harlby.

'I have been very sensible. Mr

Harlby requires no kindness from me,' Frances said chillingly. That Mrs Gaston should presume to put her much be-ringed slender fingers into this delicate affair, stung and irritated the girl to an unreasonable extent. Intuitively she felt that, however unworthy a momentary false step had rendered Herbert Harlby of her, he was at least deserving of a higher type of partizan than the woman who was his temporary ally, not out of regard for his interests, but out of dislike to the widow, whose counter influence she (Mrs Gaston) wanted to weaken.

CHAPTER II.

JOHN TREVILLE was still at Gunwalloe when Mr Harlby came back from that fruitless mission which Mrs Gaston had beguiled him into adventuring upon.

It was getting late in the afternoon when the master of the house returned to it, but though John Treville had spent the hours with Mrs Harlby alone, they had not

23

seemed long. She had proved herself a pleasant entertainer and an
admirable listener. She had treated
him with flattering cordiality as a
man, and with intelligent respect as
an inventor. He was not accustomed
to enlarge upon his favourite subject
to women. The unappreciative, not
to say stupid, remarks some of them
had made in their endeavours to
prove to him that they had grasped
his meaning, made him chary of
casting his pearls before them. But
Mrs Harlby listened patiently, comprehended quickly, and fully appre-
ciated the advantages that were
likely to result from his mechanical
efforts.

With it all she was intensely
womanly. He would have been just

enough to feel gratified by her interest in the matters wherein he had striven to arouse it, even if she had displayed it in a merely business-like way. But he was undoubtedly better pleased that she should seem to appreciate the thought and skill which had conceived and created more keenly than she did the creations themselves, and their inevitable results.

Moreover, he had never realised how dull and colourless his bachelor life at Wingates had been until the departure of the aunts. Frances and Rose Harlby threw him back upon it. The contrast between the constant cheery, graceful, pleasant presence of these four ladies in his house, with his own dismal solitude

when they left him, was damping
and depressing. For the first time he
understood that he was living merely
half a life, and a selfish one at that.
He had no one's comfort and happiness to consider more tenderly than
he did his own. When he had
taken care that his labourers were
decently housed, and that there should
be full employment for every working hand on the estate, his respon-
sibilities seemed to have come to
an end, and he felt a craving for
some of his own to look up to and
depend and rely on him. If he had
been lucky enough to possess a niece
whom he could have adopted and
taken to his own home, he would
have been quite content to make her
the head centre of his domestic life.

But the only niece he had was the daughter of a sister who was many years his senior, and she had inherited from her father a profound aversion to her Uncle John. This aversion was a groundless one in the girl's prejudiced mind, but in her father's case it was founded on the fact that, for his sister's sake, John Treville had once rescued Pottinger from the disgraceful consequences of an imfamous scrape. The benefited man never forgave his benefactor, and never ceased to depreciate and disparage him. He was a fine fellow, physically, this Major FitzJames Pottinger, exuberantly good - looking, dashing and distinguished in style. A well - born man, with a bred manner, that had made his wife his

slave from the day he first singled
her out as the object of his temporary attentions.   These temporary
attentions had been turned into
permanent ones by the stern fixity
of will of Alice Treville's father.   But
the old man's determination that his
daughter should not be spoken of
as a jilted girl, never met with any
sympathy or support from his son
John.   He would have gladly seen
the whole affair at an end.   But
his father ruled at Wingates in those
days, so Alice married her FitzJames
Pottinger, and when he got into
the infamous scrape already alluded
to, her brother John picked him out
of the mire, and wiped him as
clean as was possible for her
sake.

The daughter of this pair had most of her father's bad qualities, and all her mother's weak ones. She disliked her uncle, because her father sneered at and ridiculed the sound common sense and practicality which had got him out of the aforesaid scrape. She despised him, John Treville, because he turned a deaf ear to the incessant appeals for money, which her feeble mother was goaded into making, in order to grapple with her husband and daughter's extravagancies. Further, she detested Wingates as a dull, desolate, out-of-the-way place, with no garrison-town in easy reach of it. Accordingly, John Treville, who perfectly comprehended all this, had long ago given up the idea of making his

niece Alice the angel in his house,
for whom he was unconsciously longing.

They had drifted from a discussion
on the ascertained merits of two or
three of his recent, but still unpatented,
inventions into a conjectural one on
the subject of their monetary success,
and the steps which it would be most
advisable for him to take, in order
to secure this with promptitude. She
had opposed his half - formed intention
of 'trying some local man,' however
'good'—in other words, prompt, push-
ing and solvent — the latter might
be.

'You have always found the bigger
the market the better the business, I
am sure? I have heard you say so
often when I was at Wingates. Why

didn't you go to Paris again with your wares?'

'I am not a sentimentalist, but somehow or other I don't care to go to the house where I met Miss Woodford first.'

'But you could transact business with your friend without going to his private house?'

'If I did, he would understand the reason why, and think me a sentimental old fool.'

'Then why not take them to London?'

'I shall do so eventually, of course, only I'm feeling rather torpid and averse to moving away among strangers just at present. I know no one in town.'

'After to-morrow you will have a

very warm and hearty friend in London!'

He half smiled and shook his head.

'You're as reckless in promising good gifts as any fairy god-mother.'

'I only promise certainties. After to-morrow I shall be back in town.'

How his face glowed, and his eyes deepened with feeling, when she spoke those words of common - place kind-ness. She realised pitifully what a lone, loveless life the man must have led, when a few words of these womanly cordiality affected him so strongly.

'You mean to say that you will let me call on you? That is good of you, but I won't make the mistake of thinking that it's anything but goodness which makes you promise me a welcome. My ways won't be your ways. What should a quiet rough - diamond, such as I am, do among the gilded youth by whom you will be surrounded? Why, I even felt a bit out of place among the fine - feathered flock Harlby has had down here for the last fort-night.'

'I should think you did feel out of place among them; so did I.'

'You were the best and most beautifully feathered of them all, though not the "brightest," you left the mingling of astounding colours to Miss Hunter and the rest.'

'They mingled their colours very

harmoniously,' she said magnanimously. She was pleased though that he had declared her to be the 'best and most beautifully feathered of the flock.'

'We are wandering from our point. You must come up to London about these patents very soon, and you must come and see me very often.'

'And if I do that, do you think I shall come back and find Wingates a happier and more cheerful home than I find it now? Don't you think that I shall be risking a great deal in breaking up the grey monotony of my life and letting the sunshine in for a time only.'

'Why should it be "only" for a time? We can all make a little sunshine for ourselves if we are well and well-off, and the people we love and like live.'

'The people I love are very quickly numbered; the people who love me are fewer still. I never knew—or rather I never thought till lately—that I'm one of the loneliest fellows on earth.'

'And now that you have told me that I shall be miserable about you till I hear that you are not lonely any longer. Perhaps, who knows? my wish may be gratified sooner than we—either of us—think now. We have *both* taken it for granted that there can be but one result to Mr Harlby's meeting with Miss Woodford to-day. Supposing we are mistaken? Supposing he either proposes to her and she refuses him, or that he does not propose at all, though he loves her very much, I know."

'Even then! if she has thought of him, she won't think of me after that,' he said gloomily.

'Oh! I don't know! we women are funny creatures. Some of us do at rare times know what is best for us.'

There was a strange little break in her voice, a sudden blush on her face, a look half of confusion half of satisfaction in her eyes as they looked away towards the little postern-gate. John Treville turned his head in the same direction, and saw Harlby coming towards them with a puzzled, disconcerted expression that was a novel feature in his case.

'You're the man I want to see, Treville,' he began. Then he paused, and forced himself to smile rather drearily as he addressed Rose,—

'You will be sorry to hear that I tried my chance again to-day with Miss Woodford for the last time.'

'And she?' Rose questioned eagerly.

'Has refused me. Treville I want to tell you a long story. Come along to the library; Mrs Harlby will excuse us, I know.'

'She's a beast of a girl to have done it?' Rose said aloud in her anger as the two men walked out of earshot, 'after I have taught myself to positively *wish* for it too!'

It was but the other day that she had let herself hope Mr Harlby would turn to her for consolation if he failed to win the girl he wanted. But now she felt very glad that he had

selected John Treville for his con-
fidant instead of herself. Taking Mr
Treville's feelings into brief consideration Rose felt that he would be a
better adviser than she herself would
be. Treville would certainly not be
as anxious for the match as she was
beginning to feel, therefore he would
probably be more impartial. At anyrate
Treville would not call Frances Woodford 'a beast of a girl' for having
refused Harlby, as Rose had done in
her inconsistent wrath a few moments
ago.

'How funny it is that both these
men should want her so much when
she shows she cares for neither of
them!' Rose thought, but Rose did
not know quite all that was in the
mind of her unintentional rival, ac-

cordingly she continued to ruminate more in anger than in sorrow over the inconsistencies of her (Frances') actions.

CHAPTER III.

SELF-BLINDED.

THE long story which Harlby had taken John Treville into the library to hear took a long time in the telling. It was eight o'clock before it, and the discussion which arose out of it, came to an end. Then the first dinner-bell rang, and John Treville rose and looked at his watch.

'An hour later than I thought,

Harlby. The time has not been wasted, though. I always thought you were a good fellow, now I know you're one of the best fellows living.'

'And Frances Woodford thinks me an impostor, and my life a fraud! You must dine with us, Treville. Nonsense, man! Never mind your coat; Rose is the only lady, and she won't regard the cut of your coat more than I shall.'

John Treville tried hard to excuse himself from staying, but he did it half-heartedly. He would not for all he was worth have shown the shadow of disrespect to Mrs Harlby, especially after hearing the story which his host had just told him. But he found himself wishing to see her again, and the prospect of a *tête-à-tête* with her in the semi-seclusion of the big drawing-room, after dinner, had an inexpressible charm for him. He thoroughly understood that it was probable he would have to go out again and remain in the cold. Nevertheless, the prospect of a little temporary warmth appealed to the little that was self-indulgent and pleasure-loving in his nature.

So it was that his refusal to stay and dine with them that night was spoken in such a half-hearted way, that Mr Harlby peremptorily overruled the faint objection John Treville raised against dining in morning dress. The fact was, Harlby clung to the protection of his friend's presence, now that the latter knew everything that was to be known about his antecedents, present position, and the means and rights by which he had laid claim to and won Gunwalloe.

When Rose came down from looking at her boy after dinner, she found Mr Treville in the drawing - room alone.

' The others are playing billiards,' he explained. ' I thought I'd come here and finish our chat, if you'll have me.'

' Gladly. We are friends, you know, and, being friends, we needn't apologise for wanting to see a great deal of each other. Besides, I wanted to see you alone specially to-night. I want to ask you if you can tell *me* the story Herbert Harlby took you away to hear?'

He shook his head.

'Not to-night — not yet. He will tell it to you himself in good time.'

She blushed, and looked disappointed.

'He is not thinking of—I mean, he can have no story to tell me which I might not hear at once. Do believe me, Mr Treville, the interest I take in Herbert — the *only* interest I take in him — is as sisterly as if we had been born of the same parents.'

'That's right — that's just as it should be,' he cried heartily. 'That's the interest he wants you to take in him — that's the interest you have a *right* to take in him.'

'Don't puzzle me more than I am already,' she pleaded.

And then, like a woman, she harked back to a point which had been all-important to her once.

'It wouldn't have been so *very* odd, would it, if I had taken a deeper interest in him than a fraternal one? And it wouldn't have been an un-natural thing if he had thought of solacing himself with me, now that Frances Woodford has proved herself such a capricious, hard-natured, nasty girl?'

'It would have been unnatural to a certain extent; I can't explain to what extent just yet,' he said hurriedly. 'And as for Frances, she will make it up with him fast enough when once she knows the story he told me to-

night. As for her being hard-natured,
capricious, and nasty, she's nothing of
the sort. I should quarrel with
anyone but you who called her such
things. She's a real good, true girl,
full of the best pride a woman can
have—'

'Then why doesn't she marry Herbert, and make him happy, and
exercise her goodness and truth
and proper pride on his behalf?'

'Because— Well, she can't—being
what she is — marry him until she
knows something that he has told me
to-day.'

'Why hasn't he told her?'

'Because he has been too affectionate a son, too tolerant a brother,
and too honourable a man to secure

his own happiness by blackening others.'

'Too tolerant a brother! He has no brothers or sisters?'

'He had one brother.'

'What became of him?'

'He died. I am not going to say a word on the subject. Wait, in time I hope to persuade Harlby to do justice to himself.'

'When you look like that I know I may wheedle in vain; you'll lock your lips and defy any key of mine to unlock them. But, really, I am not so very curious about Herbert's reasons for making a secret of something. If I were Frances Woodford I should take the dear fellow for himself, and not trouble myself about any mysteries that concerned either his parents or his brother. Do urge him to take her into his confidence —at least, if it is an honourable one?'

She said the last words in an apologetic questioning way as if a buried fear had broken its grave bonds and confronted her.

'It is an honourable one, as you say,' John Treville answered, cheerfully. He did not fathom the fears which the warm-hearted, quick-witted pretty woman before him had been employed in endeavouring to chase out of their lurking places in her mind since she had come to love Herbert Harlby as a sister.

She drew a deep-relieved breath.

'Thank God! I like to hear you speak so, though, of course, I *know* that any secret he held, or confidence he made, must be honourable. I wonder if the brother, whose memory he is so tender about, was worthy of any sacrifice he has made, was a bit like him in fact?'

' Not a bit.'

' Did you know the brother, then?'

'Not at all. If I had known him I should probably have kicked him.'

' Then you know something about him—something bad? He *must* have been unlike Herbert.'

'As unlike as—as you are unlike one of the worst women I ever heard of.'

' The worst woman I ever met with wasn't so very bad,' Rose said, thoughtfully. ' She was mean and

cruel to me, because she used to say
things, that made him think less of
me, to my husband. But then, you
see' (this very humbly), 'I ought to
be ashamed of myself for admitting
it, but I didn't care very much what my
husband thought of such minor matters
as my dress and manners, and my want
of smartness and spirit and recklessness,
as soon as he began contrasting me
with *her* to my disadvantage.

'If I had known him do that I
should most certainly have kicked him,'
John Treville said, abstractedly, following out a train of thought which
she had not grasped.

'Ah! no, he wasn't worth it — I
mean he couldn't help finding me
rather flat after the brilliant women
who flattered him.'

Her tormenting owner was gone forever out of her way. She could afford to be lenient to the lash that could never cut into her purity and pride again. She felt almost kindly towards him and the lady whips who had assisted him in flaggelating her, for the mere suggestion of this conduct of theirs evoked more of John Treville's healthy, wholesome, manly sympathy for herself.

'You mustn't put him in the same category with Herbert Harlby's brother. You mustn't feel like wishing to have been able to kick him?' she said, half in earnest and half in jest. 'He had the faults of the age, and the age has such a lot of faults that we can't all hope to be free from them. I think you are,' she added abruptly,—

'I think you are quite free from what I have been told are the "faults of the age?"'

He smiled grimly. To hear this young creature speak casually of the faults of the age,' of which she knew even less than he did (blessed ignorance!) gave him a delicious transitory sense of superiority. He looked at her, and the sense of superiority vanished.

She was holding up a panel portrait of a woman in flesh-coloured tights with a fringe of fire-fraught beads dangling from her waist.

'He wrote a piece once called " The Daughter of Herodias," and wanted me dance in it dressed like *that*. When I wouldn't do it, he came home one night and told me my prudish scruples had been the making of him, as the woman with the handsomest legs in New York had kicked them about that night for his bene-fit—'

'Don't recall, don't recall,' John Treville interrupted, hurriedly. 'For-get, forget that nightmare, and begin life afresh for yourself and your boy.'

He came over close to her side, and held out his hand.

'I can't take it in anything but friendship till I know Herbert's story, and why you would have "kicked" my husband if you had known him. You will tell me these things in time, John, and till that time comes, I can just be your friend and Herbert Harlby s, and Gerald's mother, and—

yes, Frances Woodford's friend, too, if she'll let me be, and — nothing more.'

She dropped his hand, and as she did so a servant came in with a message from his master.

'Would Mr Treville come to the library. Mr Harlby wanted to speak to him at once.'

Naturally, John Treville obeyed the summons, and equally naturally, Rose tortured herself into a nervous headache in the vain attempt to fathom 'the reason why' it had been sent. She would not degrade herself by questioning a servant. But, oh, how she did long for second sight.

When John Treville joined his host in the library, at the latter's request,

Mrs Pollard looked, in the subdued light of the much lamp-shaded room, ready to meet him.

CHAPTER IV.

'FIERCE AND VAIN.'

MRS POLLARD was in one of her most florid moods. Stagnation had set in for her for several days after Mrs Gaston had sprung the black bag and its secret pocket at Mr Harlby. Nothing, to the best of Mrs Pollard's knowledge, had come of the sensational entanglement which had promised so well. The woman she had assisted

('befriended' was the word she used
in speaking of the matter to herself and
hearers), and the man whom she had
valiantly endeavoured to defame and
injure for no reason whatever, had
both alike left her in the dark as to
the result of her mischievous meddl-
ing. During these days of outward
stagnation, her mind had been very
busy evolving and maturing a plan,
by means of which she could bring
all the players in the game, about
which she felt curious, together again
under her own eyes. At last she had
an inspiration. She had a high
opinion of her own histrionic powers
and talent for organising theatricals
and tableaux. She had heard from
Mrs Gaston of that lady's brilliant
success as a dancer, and determined

to secure her for a skirt dance at least. She (Mrs Pollard), being the proud possessor of what she conceived to be a remarkably fine figure and strikingly massive limbs, thought there would be a golden opportunity of displaying these beauties fully in a piece called 'The Queen of Love,' which had been writen for her by a dramatic transient admirer when she was a decade younger, and several stone slimmer.

Of this dramatic admirer, of 'The Queen of Love' and of his wife's single appearance in it, many years ago, before an amused and slightly-shocked suburban audience, Doctor Pollard knew nothing. He had no time to read the play when she now proposed putting it on for the amusement of their friends and neighbours, and the question of costume never occurred. His sole objection to her proposal was, that 'it would turn the house inside out to have private theatricals in it.' An objection she promptly overcame by saying, 'I will ask Mr Harlby to let us do them at Gunwalloe, and if he is disagreeable and refuses, I will fall back upon Wingates. The drawing-room at Wingates will make a charming little theatre.

Accordingly, this night, finding her husband was going to Gunwalloe to see a servant who was ill, she offered to go with him to moot her plan to Mr Harlby. This she did with much volubility and no little eloquence, for her heart was very much set on taking the part of a statue of Venus with whom an impassioned poet with poetical short-sightedness falls in love.

The leading idea of the piece, as Mrs Pollard was fain to admit, was not strikingly original. Pygmalion and Galatea had been heard of before her quondam lover wrote ' My Queen of Love.' The situations, too, lacked the charm of complete novelty. But the way the statue was made to stand in divers alluring positions was unique. The suggestion was, that the poet's love had at times the power to warm the supposititious marble into life and action. There was another suggestion, that of drapery. But this was very slight.

' This hard-hearted man won't let us have this lovely room for some theatricals, we, my husband and I, are getting up for the benefit of the fund for erecting a drinking-fountain in the middle of our market-place. You, as a most abstemious man, Mr Treville, must be well aware of the inestimable service done to the cause of temperance by the erection of drinking-fountains in every town and village in the country. I am sure, therefore, that you will let us have our little entertainment at Wingates? Your beautiful long drawing-room will make a capital theatre. I read acquiescence in your eye? I knew you had the good of the masses too sincerely at heart to hesitate for a moment about granting any favour that might further the cause of their redemption from the slavery of drink.'

Mrs Pollard paused, not, it must in justice be admitted, for want of language, but from want of breath. She had, so to say, over-reached herself in her verbal fast trot. Mr Treville took advantage of the compulsory pause she made, to say deliberately,—

'I can't be responsible for what you read in my eye, Mrs Pollard, but I can assure you there is no acquiescence in my mind with your scheme as far as lending Wingates is concerned.'

'Then you show a great want of public spirit,' she replied sharply. 'We can never hope to empty the pot-houses until we have an attractive drinking - fountain in the middle of the market - square. I am quite will-ing to give the goblet and chain, but I cannot be expected to stand the whole expense of the erection.'

'Certainly not,' John Treville assented calmly.

'I have secured the services of Mrs Gaston for a skirt dance and recitation, which might be aptly introduced into the little play I have in my mind,' Mrs Pollard went on persuasively.

'What is the little play you have in your mind?' John Treville asked impassively.

'A piece that was written expressly by a very clever friend of mine, who would have been one of the leading dramatists of the day, if (poor fellow) he had only had sufficient motive to work on persistently.' She sighed heavily as she said this, and assumed an expression of remorse-ful consciousness, which sat curiously on her elderly and ruddled face.

'What's the play called? Has one ever heard of it?' John Treville asked.

'It has never been published.'

'Has it ever been played?'

'I played in it myself at the Acton Working Men's Institute some time ago,' she said loftily. 'The principal part was written expressly for me, and fits me like my skin. If it were not for Doctor Pollard's stupid and narrow prejudices, I should certainly form a company and go on tour with "My Queen of Love."'

'Is that the name of the play?' John Treville asked with a twinkle in his eye that Mrs Pollard misread and founded fallacious hopes upon.

'Yes; isn't it a charming title?' she asked eagerly, and before either man could reply she went on,—'I'm a statue of Venus in the gallery of an ardent and dreamy poet who must be romantically handsome. I won't ask either of you gentlemen to let me cast you for that part, you are both too severe for it. I can put my hand on a young man who will play it admirably. The other characters are mere nonentities. There's a chamber-maid, who is shocked at seeing the statue of Venus in her master's bed-room; and an old curmudgeon of an uncle, who threatens to cut his nephew off with a shilling unless he will dress the statue of Venus in full modern

day attire, corset, stockings and shoes
and everything. There is great fun to
be got out of that scene. The lover
has to move the statue about and bend
her limbs in order to get her clothes
on. I do the movements that gradually
become more life-like wonderfully well
everyone said, and finally, as a fashion-
ably-dressed beauty I fall into my
poet's arms and confess that I have
been flesh and blood and not marble
all along. The piece is slight, but
full of possibilities.'

'Very full, I should say. Has
Pollard seen you in it?'

'No; I have asked Mrs Gaston
to make Miss Woodford play the
prudish chambermaid, and you will do
admirably for the cranky, conventional
old uncle, Mr Treville. Now, tell

me that we may do it at Wingates?'

He shook his head in a decidedly
negative manner that showed her further
appeal for Wingates would be use-
less.

'Can you suggest any other place?'
she asked, with as imperiously impatient
an air as if he were responsible for
the plan and its fulfilment.

'There's a good long room at the
County Lunatic Asylum. I should think
that would make a very good theatre
for your operations,' John Treville
said, without the slightest emphasis that
could justify her in supposing the
suggestion was not made in perfect
good faith.

'I'll think about it. I'll make the
doctor ask for it. I have no doubt the

governors will lend it, if we offer to do the play a second night for the benefit of the asylum.'

'I don't know. The managers are sane enough, I believe; but if Pollard asks for the room for such a purpose his example may become contagious; they may all lose their heads.'

'*I* see nothing out of the way in either the play or my scheme,' she began vehemently. Then, remembering she had an object to gain which a display of viragoish fireworks were not likely to forward, she continued, with a relapse into the reasonably argumentative manner, 'You cannot possibly have any objection to helping the cause by taking the part of the uncle. Sir Galahad himself could play it without a qualm.

You will let me count on you, won't you?'

'No, I should be sorry to see the wife of my old friend Pollard make a fool of herself.'

'*Mr* Treville!'

'You may flare up as much as you like at me,' he said, with dogged contempt; 'but I will say to your face what everyone else will say behind your back. *You*, at your time of life, and with your figure, in the part of an undraped statue of Venus will be a sight for sane and decent men to fly from, and for bad and unscrupulous to jeer at—'

'And why, pray? I am not as young as I was, perhaps' (this admission was made grudgingly), 'but I am not a skinny, haggard-looking woman as so many women who are past their first prime are—'

'What's all this about?' Dr Pollard's voice was heard inquiring in a bewildered tone. 'What's this about undraped statues and your not being skinny? You certainly aren't that, my dear Auguste,' the good-natured fellow went on with a jovial chuckle; ' but what's it all about?'

There was a brief silence, broken eventually by Mr Harlby, who was inwardly seething with wrath at the presumption which had prompted Mrs Pollard to include Frances Woodford in such friskily, fatuous programme.

'Treville has been trying to persuade Mrs Pollard that its rather late in the day for her to play the Queen of Love in tights.'

There was a quickly suppressed exclamation of annoyance from Dr Pollard, and John Treville smiled grimly. Mrs Pollard glanced furtively in her usual sidelong way at the man whose description of her possible appearance had evoked these expressions of feeling from her husband and Mr Treville, and as she glanced she swore inwardly that the fraudulent impostor should rue the day he had been fool enough to cross swords with her. But she held her vindictiveness down for the present, sufficiently to be able to say with a jarring, metallic laugh,—

'The real old stock of Harlbys have always been notorious for their chivalry and courtesy towards ladies. How well you carry on the traditions of your race, Mr Harlby. Come, Dr Pollard, my patience is really exhausted. You must have passed the time more pleasantly with the sick scullery - maid than I have with her master and his local-minded friend. They both seem to think that if a woman proposes doing anything that the purblind and beclogged parochial Mrs Grundy has never heard of, that she is a fit object for their dunderheaded distrust and their blundering bucolic wit.'

She flung up her head, and almost snorted as she flounced out of the room, her skirts surging in advance of her in a way that was peculiar to them when their wearer was taking arms against the unwary who had failed to agree with her.

Dr Pollard lingered behind for a moment only. He was too discreet to say a word, but he looked with comical deprecation from one to the other of his friends, winked, and followed his wife before she had time to conjure up a vision of his conspiring against her.

There was silence in the room for a minute or two. Then the two men looked at one another and laughed long and with evident enjoyment.

'It's very gratifying to be compelled to tell such a woman as that the truth about herself for once,' said John Treville, with a look of disgust succeeding the transient one of mirth. 'Paugh! it makes a man thank God that his mother was a purblind and beclogged disciple of the local Mrs Grundy.'

'It makes a man wish that Ninon D'Lenclos had been afflicted with gout, corns and asthma before her grandson set the pernicious example to posterity of a boy falling in love with his grand-mother. I have seen many a sicken-ing spectacle in the course of my life, but that of a silly old woman trying to lure a young fellow into fancying himself in love with her is the most revolting. Someone ought to give Miss Woodford a hint not to mix herself up with this ancient tinted Venus and her infernal follies and theatricals.'

'That someone had better be yourself,' John Treville said tenta-tively.

' My good fellow, how can I — after having been distinctly rejected, and not left with the shadow of an excuse for presenting myself before her, or writing to her again? Now, you she regards as a friend still, at anyrate; and if I'm not mistaken, you regard her very much as you did when I knew you first.'

' I'm not so sure about that,' said John Treville.

Then the effulgence of a happy thought overspread his brown, plain, good face, and he added, — ' Why not get Mrs Harlby to speak to her? Give her a hint to keep clear of Mrs Pollard and all her works.'

' Yes; dear little Rose shall be our ambassadress,' Harlby assented quickly.

And apparently there was nothing re-
pellant to Treville in the other man's
use of the familiarly-affectionate phrase.

CHAPTER V.

'BUT—HAS HE?'

She hardly liked to admit it to herself, but, in reality, Frances had a strong feeling of unwillingness to leave the neighbourhood of the man whom she had insulted by her suspicions, refused to marry, and—loved as she had never loved human being before!

It was not solely her passion for independence which made her resist her aunt's entreaties to go to Bath and be comfortable, well cared for, and dull! It was quite as much a longing to see Herbert Harlby again which kept her at Cawsand with Mrs Gaston, and caused her to bear the yoke of that lady's patronage and companionship as patiently as she did.

Deep in her heart lay buried the hope that some day pride and rectitude, honour and courage would assert their dormant sway over Harlby's soul, and rouse him to make the only atonement she could ever bring herself to recognise or accept. In the meantime she could not destroy the germ of interest in the sinner sufficiently to voluntarily depart from his borders, and go into some far country where she would never have a chance even of hearing about him.

So she stayed on with Mrs Gaston, fulfilling the arduous duties of paid companion to a clever fool to the best of her ability. Listening with civility to the apocryphal stories of that lady's powers of magnetic attraction for the other sex, and being all the time, happily for herself, half unconscious of the sound, and utterly oblivious to the sense of them.

She was so absorbed in her unceasing efforts to solve the problem of Herbert Harlby's conduct that she took very little heed of what was happening around her. Mrs Gaston would leave her for whole, long summer days quite alone, while she (Mrs Gaston) was following up some more or less lively intimacies which she had formed with men who were quartered at Tregantle, Maker and Plymouth. Frances would float dreamily half the day in a little boat in the bay watching (against her better judgment) every yacht that passed in and out. Wondering if by any chance the *White Heather* would come in? And hoping (also against her better judgment) that it would do so with its owner on board.

Mrs Gaston had gone her own way, independently of her companion, for several days, when she surprised Miss Woodford by asking her to 'go over to Mrs Pollard's for a rehearsal?'

'Certainly; but what are you going to rehearse?' Frances asked, with the languid interest one is apt to feel about other people's amateur dramatics.

'It's a lovely piece, quite a classical

piece, I believe,' Mrs Gaston said hurriedly. 'I'm to do a skirt dance in it, and Mrs Pollard wants you for singing chamber-maid.'

'A "skirt dance," and "a singing chamber-maid." It doesn't sound very classical?'

'Well, classical in the same way the Gilbert and Sullivan plays are classical. Classical characters do humorous things. There's an animated Venus in it, and a bard who's in love with her, and—well, you'll see for yourself to-day what it's like.'

'Where is it to be played?'

'I *believe* at Gunwalloe.'

'I don't think I can go there,' Frances said, blushing vividly.

'What nonsense! Of course, I can't tell how far your flirtation with Mr

Harlby has gone, or why one of you, I don't know which, has cooled off. But if you refuse to go to his house on such an occasion as this, in the cause of charity too, it will look just as if you were disappointed and piqued, and all sorts of things that no woman who respects herself likes to be considered for a moment.'

'Why should I be either disappointed or piqued about Mr Harlby?'

'For this reason. Everyone knows, and everyone says, that you broke off your engagement with Mr Treville on account of your (excuse me?) passion for Mr Harlby. Many people hint that that passion was unrequited. If that supposition is correct, there comes in a fair and sufficient cause for your feeling pique and disappointment.'

The words were taunting, the tone was even more so. But Frances was far too loyal to the man she loved to allow herself to be goaded into declaring that 'he had more than requited her,' or in the phraseology of the day to 'give him away.'

'You are right,' she said quietly. 'I must not give anyone — not even Mr Harlby himself — the chance of thinking that I am piqued and disappointed. Have you an acting copy of the play? Can I look over my part?'

'It was written expressly for Mrs Pollard. It has never been published. She is having the different parts copied out. You haven't much to do. Your chief scene is where you come on and find the poet dressing the statue of Venus in his chamber.

You sing a song expressing amaze-
ment and condemnation and jealousy
when you see the statue of Venus
vitalising.'

'Who takes the part of Venus?'

'Mrs Pollard!'

'Oh!'

There was no more said by either of
them about the play or the performers
in it, until two or three hours later,
when they found themselves in Mrs
Pollard's drawing-room.

That lady had palpably prepared herself and her room for their reception.
When it is said that the preparation
of both was 'palpable,' it must not be
understood that she had beautified or
gracefully arranged either. She was not
a woman to whom the beautification
or graceful arrangement of either her

person or her surroundings came naturally and readily. The only thing that
was noticeable in her sparsely furnished,
arid, and essentially sad - looking drawing-room, was the absence of dust on
books and furniture, and the aggressive
presence of stiffly - starched Nottingham
lace curtains in the windows. There
was nothing in the room that either
harmonised soothingly or contrasted
artistically with anything else. Living
in a county whose every hedge would
have supplied her with graceful fern-
fronds all the year round, the only bit
of greenery in the room was a stunted
myrtle that would have flourished in-
finitely better in the garden. With a
garden blazing with geraniums, carna-
tions, and roses, she was content to
florally decorate her room with two or

three flowers, of incongruous hues, that were pressed into close companionship in a painted French china vase, without any foliage to relieve their vivid reds, and blues, and yellows.

With her person she played the same unattractive pranks. It appeared as if she considered that she had fulfilled her whole duty to her own person, when she had tinted her hair with some metallic preparation, that had turned it tawny in some places and green in others. Her figure being tall, large, and loose, required care and thought to be bestowed upon the garments she put upon it. But they never either fitted or flowed properly, and invariably accentuated her worst points.

It was not only that her clothes were

never up to date, but that they were
the most unbecoming survivals of a
by - gone day. When she wore light-
colours that would have befitted a girl,
she looked like a fair denizen of the
Old Kent Road out for a holiday.
When she sagaciously assumed more
sombre garments, her figure looked
dowdy in contradiction to her head
and face — which were always 'arranged' with a view to the foot-lights
apparently.

On the present occasion she had
been sagacious, and had assumed a
black-satin dress, which, it is to be
trusted, had seen better days, for its
present ones were distinctly bad. Its
sleeves and waistband were too tight,
its fulness hung in wrong places, there
was a want of purpose about its bodice

fastenings, which caused wrinkles and rucks, and it was so low at the throat that it involved the wearing of a ghastly combination of imitation lace and red velvet ribbon.

However — as she was quite satisfied with her own appearance — no one had a right to cavil at it, with the exception of her husband; and he rarely looked at her.

That this woman should seriously contemplate playing the part of a statue of Venus, which had to be gradually warmed into life by a poet's love, would have brought laughter into Frances Woodford's heart, if not into her eyes and on her lips, if she herself had not been so unalterably sad, sorry, and absorbed for and by her thoughts of Herbert Harlby. As it was, it was 'all so immaterial,' she told herself, 'what silly or sinful things other people did.' While *he* remained in a position which she thought no honourable man could knowingly occupy, what the rest of the world did was of very little consequence.

So she sat silent, and seemingly acquiescent, while Mrs Pollard expounded her views as to the play, and the people to whom the various parts should be assigned, loudly and fluently.

'You sing, I am told?' she questioned, turning to Frances, 'so I have cast you for the maid-servant's part, as there is a capital song in it, as well as some smart lines. You'll have to be lively and pert, you know. I should think the part will suit you admirably.'

If this speech had been a few degrees less rude, and the manner in which it had been delivered had been a shade less insolent, Frances would have resented it and retorted. As it was she felt that to do so would be to lower herself to the level of an assailant, who would like nothing better than a verbal battle with a foe who had less command of vituperative language than she herself was mistress of. Moreover, if the play really was to take place at Gunwalloe she would not throw away the opportunity of once more seeing Herbert Harlby, and perhaps of gaining some insight into his real relations with Rose.

So she said, in a cool self-possessed way that annoyed Mrs Pollard considerably, and amused Mrs Gaston, who liked to see the doctor's overbearing wife baffled,—

'You may be quite sure that if I undertake the part I will do my best with it.'

'But I don't know yet what your best is, my good child. I am showing great confidence in you, or rather in Mrs Gaston's estimate of your abilities, in trusting you with a part at all.'

There was an insufferable assumption of intellectual, as well as social, superiority in the manner in which these words were delivered. But Frances passed it over with a fine disdain that made the woman who disliked her causelessly and unreasonably smart.

'If in your circle you can find anyone who can do greater justice to the common-place part you offer me, pray do not hesitate to cut me out of your company,' was all she permitted herself to say, but Mrs Pollard scented a hidden slight to herself and limited coterie.

'You may be quite sure that I shall not hesitate to do exactly as I think fit,' she said, in a voice that quivered with passion at being treated independently and as an equal by 'a paid companion'; then, in a suddenly assumed, falsely suave voice, affecting to ignore Frances altogether, she went on, 'The chief man's character will be played by my young friend Roland Byrne, a charming young fellow, very handsome and clever. He's immensely flattered at my thinking him good enough to act with me. But then he really has talent, and a good idea of acting, therefore he can afford not to give himself airs.'

'And who is to be the crusty uncle?' Mrs Gaston asked.

'John Treville.'

Mrs Pollard spoke the name with an arrogantly intimate air that made Frances half loathe and half laugh. She knew well what her old lover's opinion of the shifty, unreliable, vain, boastful woman, who spoke of him thus familiarly, really was, and an almost irrepressible desire to let Mrs Pollard know it also assailed her. However, she resisted the maliciously tempting assailant, and merely smiled in a cool way that raised the fiery temper of the already excited woman to white heat.

'John Treville will take the part of the old hunks of an uncle, if I can find no one better to do it,' she went on, regardless of veracity and probability in her wrathful desire to sting the girl who was not taken in by her. 'He would have liked the lover, of course, but he would never do for that part on the stage any more than he does in real life. I am told, on excellent authority, that it's quite laughable to see the lumbering efforts he has been making lately to make himself agreeable to the widow. But Mrs Harlby, I am told, has no eyes nor ears nor thoughts for anyone but Mr Harlby, so poor old John Treville sighs in vain. I tell my husband I really must find a wife for the poor old chap when I have time, some nice, sensible, middle-aged person, who will fall in with his humdrum ways.'

' Mr Treville must be strangely altered since I knew him, far better than *you* possibly can, if he takes a wife of your choosing,' Frances said, looking her heartless persecutor full in the face.

' It really is hardly becoming of you, Miss Woodford, to refer in a boastful way to an engagement which all his *friends* know he was only too glad to be released from. I hoped you would have had the good taste to avoid the topic. I hoped you would not have forced me to tell you that Mr Treville has spoken of you to me in a way you would not feel flattered at if I could bring myself to repeat it.'

Then Frances rose to her moral, mental, and physical heights.

'I should neither feel flattered nor the reverse by anything you told me that Mr Treville had said of me to you. I should simply not believe it. I must now ask you to put the part you have assigned to me in other hands. When you malign a man like Mr Treville, by insinuating that he is a backbiter and a traitor, to a woman for whom he has always professed friendship, you prove yourself to be as dangerous as you are meddlesome and interfering.'

'When she said this she walked out of the room and out of the house, and though Mrs Pollard flung her head up and laughed boisterously, she did so with an unsmiling face. She had been worsted, and she hated the woman who had worsted her only a few degrees more than she did the one who had witnessed, and was politely enjoying, her discomfiture.'

'What do you think that creature will do now?' she asked.

And Mrs Gaston answered gaily,—

' Impossible to say; but I should think that she is very likely to go straight to Wingates, and tell Mr Treville that you charge him with defaming her.'

' And how will he prove that he has not? for I can swear that he always said these things about her when he and I were alone,' Mrs Pollard cried triumphantly.

' But—has he?'

'Of course he has! If I say so!'

And then the sound of a wickedly
vindictive laugh echoed round the
room, and Mrs Gaston silently con-
gratulated herself on never having
made a single genuine confidence to
this stirrer-up of strife.

CHAPTER VI.

A DEAD OBSTRUCTION.

FRANCES walked rapidly down the
street of the little country town, away
from the atmosphere of the woman
who had been powerless to move her
to retort, until (mean last resource!)
that woman had attacked the honour
of the man for whom Frances had a
feeling of well-founded and unutterable
loyalty and regard. It was attacking
his honour, attacking it in the most

subtly vile way, to hint that he had stooped so low as to speak slightingly of herself—Frances Woodford!

Every instinct within her told her that he, the good, staunch, true gentleman, was incapable of having done this degrading thing. Yet there had been such assurance in Mrs Pollard's words and manner, that more than once Frances caught herself thinking the very same words which Mrs Gaston had spoken.

'But—has he?'

She breathed more freely, and the mists of the doubt of him dispersed, when she got clear of the little High Street, and found herself close to the entrance to what had once been the pride and pleasure of the town, its bowling-green.

There was a large pond, railed in
on one side of the wide drive, which
swept through the arched gateway on
to the green, and on these railings
Frances leant to watch the ducks
and a swan or two steering their
course among the masses of yellow and
white water-lilies which covered half
of the area of water.

She was debating the question with
herself—that is to say, her reason and
her impulses were arguing it hotly—
as to whether she should keep silence
and allow Mrs Pollard's allegations
against John Treville to pass unrefuted
or not. Expediency, prudence, perhaps
a wise woman's natural cowardly aversion to mixing herself up with a
gossip's tale, prompted her to hold her
tongue; but, on the other hand, all

that was generous within her urged her to give him the chance of administering a check to Mrs Pollard's onslaught against his good faith and honour. As the latter lady had 'cried havoc, and let loose the dogs of war,' which were kennelled in her tongue, against him before Frances herself, it was, intuition argued, more than likely that others had been favoured with her (Mrs Pollard's) pernicious, poisonous weeds of eloquence on the subject. So she was coming to the definite conclusion that she would write to Mr Treville, and tell him frankly that the attempt had been made to induce her to believe that he had spoken of her, if not in a defamatory, at least in a depreciatory manner, by Mrs Pollard.

' I owe it to him to give him the opportunity of proving the lie—the lie it is.
There can't even be half a truth in
it!' she whispered to herself, as she
drew up from the railings on which
she had been leaning, straightening
herself with the strength of the resolu-
tion to which she had come. As she
did so, two men came along the road
towards the bowling - green. One of
them held an open letter, edged with
black, in his hand, and was speaking
earnestly to his companion. With very
mixed feelings, Frances recognised and
exchanged greetings with her old and
her new lovers.

All thoughts of worrying and disturb-
ing him about such a trifle as the
gossip which had fallen from a false
woman's tongue fled from her mind as

she looked at John Treville's haggard, anxiety - lined face, and observed how the hand which held the black-edged letter trembled. Her one thought now was to offer him the sympathy which she felt he still deserved from her, and give him comfort if she could. Thrilled as she was by the mere presence of the new lover, the distress of the old one commanded her keenest current interest.

She gave Mr Treville time to collect himself by explaining to Herbert Harlby the cause of her presence in the little town, adding,—

'But I found I should not be in sympathy with either the play or the players, so I have resigned my part, and begged Mrs Pollard to find a substitute for me.'

'I am very glad of that,' Harlby said heartily. 'Neither Treville nor I would be mixed up with it in any way, and I am afraid I should have presumed to interfere and advise you to have nothing to do with it, if you had been led into promising to join them.'

'Mrs Pollard relies on you, I think, for the part of the uncle,' Frances said, looking at Mr Treville, who was still holding the letter in his hand, looking at it now and again with a deepening expression of perplexity.

'Who, I?' he asked, coming out of his reverie with an effort. 'Indeed, I wouldn't have had any part or lot in the affair, but now *this* has happened' (he glanced at the letter again) 'it is doubly impossible.'

'You have had sad news?' she asked softly.

'More than sad — bad, terribly bad,' he answered roughly, but there was no roughness in the quick look of grateful appreciation which he shot at her. 'My sister's husband has just—died in a most dis — tressing way, and God only knows what will be the end of it for us all.'

'I am *so* sorry for you,' she said, taking his hand, and making no attempt to conceal the tears which had sprung to her eyes in response to his tone, more than his words, of despairing misery. She knew what John Treville's opinion of his brother-in-law had always been, and fathomed that it was something worse than Major Pottinger's death which had broken down the strong, self - contained man so completely.

'You may as well hear the whole story. It is in the London papers already. It will be in the local ones to - morrow,' he said, more broken-heartedly than bitterly. 'He has died in a drunken row with another blackguard about a woman, who has been fool enough, poor thing, to kill herself on his account. There's a suspicion of foul play about her death, and a suggestion that he committed suicide to avoid consequences—'

'In this letter—is this letter the first you have heard of it?' Frances interrupted eagerly.

'Yes, this is the first intimation I've had of it. My poor sister is nearly mad. She loved that scoundrel through all his infamous life, and is breaking her heart over his loss now as hopelessly as if he had been the best, kindest and most faithful husband in the world.'

'Poor thing! don't blame her for her fidelity,' Frances said compassionately. 'The letter telling you all this is not from her?'

'Oh, no, no! it's from a friend of hers, who has always tried to prove her devotion to poor Alice by pitching into Pottinger.'

'Then most likely she exaggerates things now and paints facts in the blackest colours.'

'No, she doesn't; she's an awfully accurate woman, with no malice, only with an extraordinary amount of candour about her. But it's too bad of me to bother you with my troubles. I've no doubt you have enough of your own.'

'We all have our full share, I fancy,' Harlby put in quietly. 'But that's no reason why we shouldn't bother, as you call it, about the troubles of a friend.'

'After all,' Frances said wistfully, wishing for his sake that she had the right to give fuller comfort and sympathy to John Treville, — 'After all, turn away from looking at the blackest side of it, and think. In time your sister will be a happier woman than she has been, and is now. She has a daughter to console her, and if she is let mourn for him to her heart's content, fully and freely, just as if he *had* been the best, kindest and most faithful husband in the world, she will be at peace at least, for no one will be cruel enough to tell her how she died.'

'She knows it already,' John Treville gulped out, 'otherwise do you think I should feel it as I do? If it had been kept from my poor sister, I would gladly have sealed my lips about everything connected with Pottinger's life and death. But she knows what is rumoured, and in her blindness of heart she wants his memory to be defended,' wants me to bring actions for libel against the whole London press, it appears to me.'

'She will listen to reason from you. Bring her to Wingates at once, won't you?'

'She will have no other home,' he

said gloomily; 'he has died up to the hilt in debt, leaving his wife and daughter without a penny. You see my life's duty and work is cut out for me.'

He spoke so despondently, that her woman's wit told her there was more than met the eye, or could be accounted for, by the mere fact of Major Pottinger's death and his sister's consequent de pending upon him. It must surely be the downfall of some dear scheme which was making generous, kind-hearted John Treville rebel against the fate which forced him to protect and provide for his own sister and niece.

'I must go and send off a telegram now, and start for Brighton by the night-mail,' he was saying to Harlby. No place but Brighton suited his

health, he always said, so he took a
house there three years ago, and has
not spent three months altogether in
it since.   Good-bye Miss Woodford,
God bless you for your sympathy.   You
don't know how badly I need it.   Harlby, I won't take you away, you'll hear
from me in a day or two.'

'He was off before they could either
of them stop him, and then Frances said
earnestly,—

'There is something more; what is
it?'

'I may tell you I know he regards
you and your opinion more highly than
that of any other woman in the world,
though he no longer loves you the best.
Yesterday he asked Rose, Mrs Harlby,
to marry him, and she said "Yes," to my
intense gratification.   To-day this news

has come, and he is divided between two duties. He thinks his first duty is to his sister. Her home must be at Wingates, for she is absolutely unprovided for; has no head for management, and her daughter is worse. Between them they would make ducks and drakes of any income he could allow them if left to themselves, and then come to poor Treville for more.'

'Then he must let them muddle and mismanage, and make ducks and drakes of their income, and refuse them the 'more' for which they may unreasonably ask. His first duty is to the woman he has asked to marry him! How glad I am for him after all. Your news has made me almost happy again, Mr Harlby.'

She shone a smile at him, and took it quite for granted that he should walk along by her side as he was doing. In a few minutes she found herself recounting to him the episode which had occurred at Mrs Pollard's house that afternoon. It had all sank into such utter insignificance now. In the presence of John Treville's real trouble, what did it matter what a local gossip, whose tongue never wearied of wagging ill-naturedly, said or implied about him?

So she merely recounted it for the sake of supplying a reason why she had apparently so capriciously changed her front, and thrown up the part in 'The Queen of Love,' which she had gone to Mrs Pollard's house with the avowed object of taking. There was no desire on her part to arouse his championship on her behalf. It rather vexed her than otherwise when he said in reply,—

'Give me the right to protect you against such insults in the future.'

'That subject is closed between us, Mr Harlby.'

'If this wretched business about Treville's scamp of a brother-in-law had not occurred, I should have been able to satisfy your scruples about myself fully, very shortly.'

'How can his death or disgrace affect you?'

'Through Rose; if Treville can't marry, I am tongue-tied still. But, believe me, it is not on my own ac-count that I maintain a silence which destroys my only chance of happiness.'

'How can I believe you, knowing what I do?' she said sadly, and then the seldom dormant fiend of jealousy goaded her into saying,—'Mrs Harlby's interests are evidently paramount with you. I can put but one interpretation on your declaration, that if Mr Treville does not marry her, *you* are tongue-tied. We had better say good-bye, now, for I see Mrs Gaston coming in the distance, and I would rather she did not see you with me. Her raillery is not always refined, and I am not in a mood to endure it to-day.'

'The sins of the father are visited upon the children, and no mistake in my unfortunate case,' he muttered to himself, as she bowed slightly, and passed swiftly on ahead of him.

CHAPTER VII.

HEARTLESS HONOUR.

JOHN TREVILLE had been right in his melancholy forecast. The following day the local papers teemed with sensationally paragraphed and worded accounts of the probable cause and actual manner of Major Pottinger's death.

His connection with the old, well-reputed Treville family was dragged forward ruthlessly, and commiseratingly commented upon. The odium of the man's crime against the wretched woman who had taken her own life was made the theme of many a hysterical jeremiade against the irony of the fate which had linked that crime with one whose whole career had been so spotless, and who was so much respected by friends, neighbours, dependents, and the world at large, as the master of Wingates. The affair, indeed, was a godsend to the daily papers. It was better than a murder, and nearly as good as a divorce case in high life, and it was made the most of and padded out of all proportion to its real and reasonable bearing on John Treville's life and status.

It would have been impossible to

keep the daily papers out of Mrs Harlby's hands, as the library and morning - room tables literally were always brimming over with them, even if she had not been given full information on the appalling topic from another source. But as it was, John Treville had written to her, telling her as clearly and succinctly as he could exactly how the case stood. About Major Pottinger he said little, nothing extenuating, and setting forth nothing in malice. But about his sister and niece he was obliged to say a great deal.

He put vividly before Rose Harlby the helplessness of their condition, their pennilessness, their incapacity, their utter irresponsibility, and the disgrace which now attached itself to their

name. He told her that, knowing it
to be his duty to support, stand
by and protect them, he meant to
do that duty at the cost of every
consideration of self. And he ended
by telling her that hardest of all
truths for a proud, sensitive woman
to hear, that he had no alternative
in honour but to release her from
all further association with a family
that would be regarded by the world
as tainted and degraded.

She received this letter simultane-
ously with the London papers of the
previous day, and the West Country
journals of the current one, and all
of these teemed with the reports
of the " Distressing and Disgraceful
Tragedy." It was from John Treville's
letter, however, that she had the first

information of being herself interested and concerned in one of the most painful dramas of the day.

The blow fell upon her unexpectedly—such blows always do! Herbert Harlby, though he had been cognisant of what was coming, through a chance meeting with John Treville in the little post-town the day before, had shrank with a human being's natural shrinking from being the one to give a woman agony in order to smooth the way for another fellow's explanation. He would have run any amount of personal risk and danger for either Rose or John Treville. But he was not prepared to put the knife into the former in order that the latter might be spared the onus of inflicting the first wound.

Accordingly Rose had been passing the hours of the last day, and the early morning of the present one very pleasantly with her boy, and in the society of a young daughter of the rector's, who had stayed on with her when the other lady guests departed, and her position at Gunwalloe would have been untenable otherwise.

John Treville's offer and Mr Harlby's acceptance of it could scarcely have been called public property yet, for it had not been officially announced by the man which in decent circles, is the only announcement to be relied upon. But every servant in the house saw and spoke about what 'was coming!' and Fanny Gilding, the rector's daughter, knew it.

The two girls—Rose was a girl in

years still, in spite of her widowhood
and her baby—were breakfasting together when their letters were delivered
to them. The local papers were already
lying on the table in the bay-window
of the morning-room, to which nook
everyone was accustomed to retire and
glean news as the whim seized him
or her during breakfast.

'Mr Harlby is late; isn't he coming
to have any breakfast with us?' Rose
inquired, as her letters were handed to
her.

'Master breakfasted at eight, and has
gone out—fishing,' the man answered
slowly. He had observed that there
was something amiss with his master
that morning, and, having carefully per-
used the *Western Morning News* before
he folded it neatly and placed it on

the morning-room table, he was quite prepared for the worst that might follow.

'Mrs Harlby is a proud 'un,' he had observed to one of his colleagues; 'she'll chuck that there Treville after this, you take my word for it. I should be glad to see her married to Harlby himself, if it wasn't for that kid of hers, but I don't hold with ready-made families; they're cuckoos in the nest, as a rule.'

The perceptive person who had advanced these opinions at an earlier hour lingered about the room for a few minutes, while Mrs Harlby read John Treville's letter. He altered the altitude of all the blinds; he readjusted the folds of the curtains; he hovered around, in fact, until Mrs Harlby had read her letter, and then he experienced keen disappointment.

For she drank the remainder of her coffee composedly, pressed some cream upon an anything but unwilling cat, and then rose buoyant and beautiful as ever, saying,—

'Come away to the lawn, Fanny, it's the best reading-room in the place, I think. Bring all the papers, and we'll have little Gerald out with us.'

'She's as well-plucked as she's proud,' the servant thought admiringly, as he watched the two ladies walk through the open window and up the steps that led on to the lawn that had a battlemented wall for its boundary on the seaside. 'I wish she had been master's choice instead of that grim-faced Treville's. But then

there's that kid; and we don't rightly
know who its father was. But she *is*
a well-plucked one.'

She was a 'well-plucked one' truly,
for though she was smarting cruelly
under what she conceived to be John
Treville's ready renunciation of her
for the gratification of his over-strained
sense of honour, she gave her companion no hint of her being other
than the cloudless-minded happy woman
she had been previously in reality.

With feminine outspokenness she had
told Fanny Gilding of the great con-
tentment and happiness she felt in
the prospect of becoming Mr Treville's
wife. She had made no mystery about
the affair; she had felt no mock bash-
ful reticence about it. He had made
open mention of it at once to his

greatest friend, Harlby, and had even suggested to her that she should tell Fanny before the latter heard a hint of it from anyone else. This had only been two days ago. And now he had written not to 'offer' to release her, but to release her and himself from their mutual vows without giving her the option of appeal.

It was a cruel, stinging blow, and it cut into her pride as if she had been slashed with a cat-o'-nine-tails. Secure in the possession of wealth of her own that was sufficient, and more than sufficient for all the needs that either she or little Gerald could ever have, she did not take into account the weight her wealth would lay upon John Treville's shoulders if he took it with her and gave her nothing in return but himself. She did not take into account either the manly shrinking he felt against bringing her bright, unclouded spirit into the fellowship that a residence under the same roof would enforce with the broken, helpless, hopeless woman to whom Major Fitzjames Pottinger had left nothing but a disgraced name. It seemed to Rose that the reasons he assigned, and the arguments he brought forward for setting her free, were only so many shallow excuses for getting rid of her. Accordingly, she resolved to accept his dictum without a word or sign of regret, and to let him pursue his selfish bachelor way alone, without let or hindrance from her.

It seemed to her that she was destined to be plucked and then care-

lessly thrown aside by every man. First
of all, her husband had taken her care-
lessly, without ever making an effort
either before or after marriage to win
her love, respect or confidence. Then
the other Herbert Harlby had been,
and still was touchingly, tenderly, chival-
rously devoted to, and thoughtful for
her. Her heart had been very warmly
ready to go out to him at one time,
but obviously he had not coveted the
treasure, for he had not only never
asked for it, but had told her of his
unalterable, though unavailing love for
another woman. Lastly, had come John
Treville, with his heart of gold in a
plain casket, with his patient endurance
of the sorrow Frances Woodford had
caused him, and finally with his half-
doubting prayer that the pity she (Rose)

felt for him and his loneliness, might deepen into something stronger, and centre in him, banishing that loneliness, enriching and enlarging his life.

She had listened to that prayer; she had dispelled that doubt; she had let herself revel in the reflection that at last she had found true sanctuary in a *real* man's heart. And—this was the end of it; this was the end of such a common-sense romance that surely it *might* have lasted.

CHAPTER VIII.

A CLEVER ADVOCATE.

WITH her mind full of the thoughts that have been crudely described, Mrs Harlby nevertheless contrived to keep up an animated appearance of interest in Gerald's immature efforts to walk and talk, and seemed to listen to the scraps of news which Fanny Gilding gave out in a desultory way.

'This is a dull paper,' the girl said impatiently ; 'there's literally nothing in it but politics, and sporting announcements and accounts of the opening of chapels in Widger Street, and long speeches by various M.P.'s about Home Rule and the inefficient state of the navy. Not a word about fashion or the royal family, or Lady Mingleton's divorce, or anything amusing. Oh! What's this?'

She had come across a paragraph in the London Letter beginning :—

'The lamentably disgraceful circumstances which preceded and attended the death of Major Pottinger are, unhappily, the one topic of conversation in all the clubs, and, indeed, in all places where men congregate. They are already hinted abroad in every London journal, and to-morrow will be published all over the land by the provincial press. It will be a

matter of deep regret to many of
your readers that such a disgrace to
manhood should have been so closely
associated, by marriage, with the old
and highly-reputed family of Treville
of Wingates.'

'Stop!' Rose cried, taking the
paper from Miss Gilding's unwilling
hand. 'You must not read that case,
Fanny.'

'Why not? Oh, Mrs Harlby, I
am so sorry! Poor Mr Treville, what
a blow it will be to him. Just as he's
engaged to you, too! It's awful for
him.'

'It is awful for him, but he is not
engaged to me.'

'Did you know of this? Have you
thrown him over because of this?'
Fanny asked eagerly.

She was seventeen, and her current ambition was to be loved by a romantic criminal to whom she would be everlastingly faithfully through much tribulation, including the withdrawal of the countenance of her family and friends.

'I knew of it this morning. I had a letter from Mr Treville telling me of this sad business, and that he wanted no more of me.'

'Do you mean to take him at his word?' Fanny asked, aghast at the idea of any woman surrendering without a struggle her claim to being mentioned in remotely innocent connection with an appalling case.

'I always take men at their word. I took Mr Treville at his word the day before yesterday, and said "yes" when

he asked me to marry him.   To-day I
take him at his word again, and, believ-
ing that he thinks it better for himself
to get rid of me, I agree to being got
rid of.   That is all.   You needn't look
so aggressively sympathetic, Fanny, dear.
He has taken the coward's refuge, and
pretends that it's for "my good" he
sets me free.   And I don't care a bit—
not *one bit!*'

She strengthened this last assertion
by breaking into angry sobs, declaring
that Gerald was making himself revolt-
ingly filthy by rolling on the grass,
catching up that unconscious nuisance
and hurrying him into the house.

As soon as she was well within its
portals, her tractable little friend, Fanny
Gilding, read through the whole of the
Pottinger case.

' There is no further reason for my staying here. Mr Treville has broken off his engagement with me,' Rose said abruptly, when Herbert Harlby came home by-and-by.

' Don't let him do anything so suicidal ; that is if you really have any regard for him,' Harlby pleaded impatiently.

It seemed to him so fatuously frivolous of these two people, if they were fond of one another, to decide on severing, now that one of them was in real thoroughgoing, downright trouble, which the other would not have dreamt of shrinking from sharing, had she been given the option of doing so.

' Why on earth should people make more misery for themselves, when there is always a good stock of it that's been made by other people handy for one's use?' he went on severely, as Rose had vouchsafed no answer to his plea.

'Is it just and reasonable of you to blame me for what Mr Treville has done of his own free will? I don't believe that his brother-in-law's bad conduct has anything at all to do with the matter. He's tired of me, or else he still has hopes of winning Miss Woodford eventually. *Everyone* likes her best.'

'Don't cry, please don't, Rose,' he begged abjectly.

It was really too trying to be cried at by a very pretty woman on account of another man.

'Don't cry! Is that all you have to say to me when you know I am going to lose the best chance of happiness I've ever had in my life? I shall go away and be quite wretched and lonely, and never speak to another man till little Gerald grows up, and then *he'll* not want me, but will fall in love with some horrid girl, who will take him away from his poor old mother.'

The fancy picture painted by herself of Rose, old, decrepit and deserted, did not touch Herbert Harlby very deeply. It was such a far-off cry. Still he infused a good deal of sympathy and soothing into his reply.

'Poor Treville was half distracted when he wrote that letter. I saw him yesterday, and the misery he felt on your account was something quite pitiful to witness.'

'On *my* account, and he causing
me the misery the whole time. No,
no, I can't believe that he felt anything but a nasty, proud, mean determination to bear the whole burden
of this—trouble quite alone. That's
just like him. That's just like all
men—I mean all men who are worth
anything.'

He refrained from using her
argument against herself, and con-
tented himself with saying dolefully,—

'Poor Treville! What a reign of
misrule there'll be at Wingates when
his sister and niece hold the reins
of household government. I shouldn't
be at all surprised if they ruin him
in the course of twelve months and
bring Wingates to the hammer.
Poor Treville!'

'You don't think anything of the kind,' she said uneasily.

'I do indeed. You know what a good, open - handed fellow he is, devoting himself to the good of others and his mechanical inventions. Luckily for him he has always had a staff of servants who are trustworthy and have his interests at heart. But they won't stay under the Pottinger *regimé*, and then he'll be at the mercy of a gang of mercenaries who will soon lay the land bare.'

'It will be his own fault,' she said waveringly.

'It will not be his own fault. It will be due to his highly-strung sense of honour, and to (excuse me) the way in which a woman's pride and

self-love allowed her to relinquish the
task of his salvation directly he hoisted
a signal of distress.'

She was getting manifestly uncom-
fortable.   She had thought that at
least Herbert Harlby would have
applauded her action in scorning
and letting another man go under
the circumstances.

'As for Miss Woodford,' he went
on manfully, disregarding any pain
he might bring upon himself by his
introduction of her name,—'As for
Miss Woodford, I can assure you
that he is too heartily in earnest in
wishing to see her married to me
for it to be possible for him to have
any lingering tenderness for her. She
never had anything but a friendly
feeling for him, and so failed to inspire

him with anything warmer than a friendly feeling for her.'

'Oh, how can you tell me that? You mean that I was bold and forward and unwomanly and *horrid*, and let him see that I liked him first.'

Her eyes flashed indignation upon him, but he did not shrink from their scorching rays in the least. He had a dearer object to gain in uniting her to John Treville even than the latter's happiness.

'I mean to say that his was the desire of the "moth for the star," until you, with *unconscious* womanly tenderness let him see that you didn't regard him as a moth, or yourself as a star. Poor old chap! Perhaps it would have been better for him if he had gone on thinking you an unobtainable star.'

'Perhaps it would have been better for both of us if he had put all the nonsense about "stars" out of his head' (John Treville had never had this nonsense in his head it may be remarked. Harlby was only ascribing the folly to him for his own, Treville's, good), 'and treated me like an ordinary woman.'

'You must see that it would be difficult for any man to do that,' he said gallantly.

'I'm not in a mood for any silly flattery,' she said loftily.

'If you hadn't stopped me you would have found the remainder of my speech anything but flattering,' Harlby said, with a pretence of being offended.

'Oh, Herbert, don't you turn against me *too!*'

'I was going to tell you that in

writing to offer to release you, because he is under a cloud, or thinks himself under a cloud, he treated you like a very ordinary woman indeed. But he thought, as I confess I did, namely, that you would rise superior to expediency, shake off the trammels of selfish prudence, and write and tell him that you are as much his for better and worse as if you were already his wife. That's what I thought you would do, Rose, and that's what I told poor Treville yesterday you would do when he was preparing to immolate himself upon the altar of your well-being in the eyes of the world.'

She turned to him doubtfully, and put up her little clasped hands to him with a gesture of confidence that would have wrung his conscience if he had not felt sure that all he had been saying to her was so very much for her own good.

'From the day I saw you first I made up my mind that I would rely on you entirely, Herbert. I made you the arbiter of my destinies. I will write as you wish to John Treville; you need not tell me what you wish. I know, and I'm sure you're right.'

CHAPTER IX.

'PHAUGH!'

THERE had been three rehearsals of 'My Queen of Love,' and not one of them had gone off comfortably ; but the outside world knew nothing of this.

'The heartless, unsympathetic outside world' was not worthy to be taken into the confidence of the *real* artistes, who, without hope of reward, were

struggling undauntedly through divers
difficulties for that world's weal.

The difficulties were enormous, and
if Mrs Pollard had not been buoyed
up by the thought of the costume
she was to wear as the statue of
Venus, she would have been overcome
by them. As it was, she overlooked
them, treated them as if they did
not exist, and only laughed when the
others wrangled over their words and
business.

At last, on the very day of the pro-
jected entertainment, a terrible thing
occurred.

They were having a dress rehearsal
in the afternoon, and though the young
lady who had been put in Frances
Woodford's original part was in tears
because the mud student, who was *her*

real lover in real life, was making such a lot of apparently unnecessary love to the statue of Venus, matters seemed to be progressing with comparative smoothness. To be sure, a note of discord would be struck presently, as Mrs Gaston meant to insist on there being three skirt dances for her introduced. She had already mooted this point privately to her friend, Mrs Pollard, and that lady had angrily demurred. But Mrs Gaston meant to dance three skirt dances, or none at all!

'If you have three dances, it will cut my life-developing scene short,' Mrs Pollard had remonstrated, and Mrs Gaston had unwarily replied,—

'If you cut that scene out altogether it would be better.'

'Who says so, besides yourself?' Mrs Pollard asked indignantly, and again Mrs Gaston was unwary.

'My dear, do you remember the reason Mr Pickwick gave to Tupman against the latter appearing as a brigand at Mrs Leo Hunter's fancy-dress party?'

'I've forgotten it,' Mrs Pollard asserted, colouring through layers of powder.

'Well, when Tupman asked, "And why should I not wear it, sir?" Pickwick simply replied, "Because you're too old, sir, and if you want another reason, you're too fat."'

'Pickwick was an underbred old man. Everyone who knows anything of English literature and English Society knows that Dickens did not intend Pickwick to be accepted as the typical English gentleman,' Mrs Pollard said lightly, turning to the young mud student. who was rehearsing the part of impassioned poet lover to her statue of Venus. 'I am afraid he would condemn Mrs Gaston's skirt dance as brusquely, not to say brutally, as he did Mr Tupman's brigand costume. We must get on with this. Prompter, what is my cue?'

'I have the three dances, or I shall be taken suddenly ill, and will not be able to appear at all,' Mrs Gaston threatened with a prettily light malicious air that thinly veiled serious mischief.

'Do your first dance as a curtain-raiser; and dance the house out then!' Mrs Pollard said resolutely.

She was beginning to hate her blithe,

grass-widow friend, more especially as the
latter's dancing had taught the developing
mud student where to look for stunning
little feet if he wanted to find them.'

'The house will never move out
while *I* dance, will it?' Mrs Gaston
was whispering to 'the boy' whom Mrs
Pollard was instructing in the histrionic
art, when the carpenter, who waited on
the company, came in with a message to
Mrs Gaston.

'Please, ma'am, there's a gentleman
outside says he's your 'usbing, and
must see you at onst.'

'Ask the gentleman to come in,'
Mrs Pollard ordered before Mrs Gaston
could grasp the situation, collect her
draperies and limbs more compactly, and
concentrate her faculties sufficiently to
reply to the message herself.

Mrs Pollard had organised the entertainment. In the carpenter's own words it was she who 'bossed the show.' Consequently her order to show the gentleman in was promptly obeyed, and in a few moments the long and pleasantly-parted husband and wife found themselves face to face.

The latter had flung her long and voluminous cloak over her shoulders by this time, and had subdued her agitation at hearing of Mr Gaston's unexpected arrival sufficiently to greet him with composure.

'You should have let me know you were coming. I would have gone to London to meet you,' she said affably, but there was little corresponding affability in either his smile or reply.

'It struck me that I should get

more satisfaction out of the very un-
affected surprise you're feeling now,
than I should have got from a pre-
meditated welcome. Besides, you might
have had a pressing engagement in
some other part of the globe which
you would have been bound to fulfil
if you had known I was coming, so
I've saved us both some trouble by
dropping in.'

'And you're just in time to see Mrs
Gaston rehearse the charming skirt
dance with which she is going to
ravish our eyes to-night,' Mrs Pollard
said enthusiastically, advancing towards
the astounded new arrival in Venus's
immaterial draperies.

'Seems to me if you did a "skirt"
walk or a "skirt" sit down it would
create a considerably more bracing at-

mosphere of propriety in this agreeable assemblage,' Mr Gaston remarked
sourly, so sourly indeed that Mrs
Pollard's always scanty stock of sweetness became acidulated at once.

'*Do* show him how you nearly cover
the stage with your swirling skirts
just before you do the high kick,
dear!' she said, going up to her friend,
who was quivering with anger and un-
certainty. Then, before the fair *danseuse*
was aware of the intention, Mrs Pollard
had clutched the shielding cloak off, and
Mrs Gaston stood revealed before her
husband's eyes in all the bravery of
miles of rainbow - hued gossamer, hanging loose from her throat to her
feet.

'Come out of this!' he said sternly,
placing his hand on her shoulder as he

spoke.   Whereat the young farming pupil giggled, it not being clear to him whether the irate husband meant her to 'come out' of her skirts, or out of the room and company in which he found her.

'You ought to be ashamed of yourself! You, a woman with children, and a married daughter in Boston, to put yourself into a thing that looks like a lunatic's night-dress, and fling your legs about in public like an inebriated marionette. And as for *you*,' he added savagely to Mrs Pollard, who was affecting to try and subdue convulsive bursts of laughter, 'as for *you*, you're twice as bad, for you're older, and you haven't the looks to tempt you to make an ass of yourself that she has.'

Mrs Pollard's mirthful mood changed

in an instant to one of malignant
spite.

'Before you insulted me so grossly,'
she raved out, with what she felt to
be her best imperious air, 'it would be
well you should remember that your
wife danced skirt dances *constantly* in
New York in dramatic entertainments,
got up by herself and her friend Mr
Harlby.'

'Her friend "Mr Harlby!" You'd
better keep those statements of yours
for feast - days and Sundays. They're
no good for everyday use.'

His obvious contempt, and the dread
that Mrs Gaston would escape further
censure, stung Mrs Pollard into a more
desperate determination than before to
be loyal to herself, and to hit everyone
else whom she dare.

'Yes, her friend Mr Harlby! The friendship, according to her own account, was such a pronounced one, that I took it for granted you knew all about it, and acquiescently kept out of the way. I am really sorry to have let the cat out of the bag,' she added condolingly to Mrs Gaston; 'it would have been *wiser* if you had confided in me more fully, then I should have been on my guard.'

'Phaugh!' said Mr Gaston, as he picked up his wife's cloak and put it over her shoulders. 'Come on, my dear,' he added kindly, 'we'll get out of this at once, and go back to that nice, smart girl who told me where I should find you.'

'Let me change my frock,' Mrs Gaston pleaded, but he shook his head, saying,—

'No, come along; I've a carriage out-side. Your maid can come and fetch anything you leave behind you here to-morrow. Here,' to the carpenter, 'are you in charge of this place?'

'Yes, sir,'

'Have you a wife?

'Yes, sir; she's been helping the ladies to—'(he hesitated, not being sure which it would be correct to say, to 'dress' or to 'undress').

Mr Gaston supplied him with the right words.

'To make guys of themselves. Well, you tell your wife to put Mrs Gaston's property under lock and key till her maid fetches them to-morrow, and give her this for her trouble.'

This being a five-pound note, that village carpenter and his wife retained lastingly agreeable recollections of the entertainment Mrs Pollard had essayed to get up, though the actual performance of it was destined never to gladden the eyes of the public.

For even now, at the eleventh hour, as it were, Mrs Pollard's scheme for giving the inhabitants such a tangible and palpable idea of Venus as they should be bound to carry in their mind's eye for some time fell through, in consequence of the intervention of the green-eyed monster!

The young lady who was to do the singing chambermaid, and her lover, the farming pupil, who was to play the poet lover, had a violent tiff in consequence of the realistic air with which the latter played his amorous part. It ended in the *fiancée* becoming hysterically unreasonable, but at the same time doggedly determined. She 'would break her engagement with him that very hour,' she said, 'unless he would throw up the part which involved his making a fool of himself with a woman old enough to be his mother.'

He nearly cried, but he did what she desired him to do, and so 'My Queen of Love' was never played at all, as Mrs Pollard found it impossible to sustain the weight of all the characters on her own shoulders, massive as these latter were.

CHAPTER X.

TREVILLE SAYS 'I WILL.'

ROSE's letter breathing the frankest friendship and the most self-abnegating, generous desire to stand by him and share in all his troubles, disgraces and expenses, reached Mr Treville while he was giddy with gazing into the abyss of debt and ruin into which Major Pottinger had plunged his unhappy wife and daughter.

For the three years during which the Pottingers had lived at Brighton, they had individually and collectively denied themselves nothing that they desired. Major Pottinger had a fine air, 'a lordly way' some of those he patronised termed it, and he never went about with what the Irish call a 'poor mouth.' He ordered everything he wanted with the accustomed confident manner that tradespeople find so reassuring. He never disgraced them by wearing ill-cut or shabby clothes in their shops, nor did he permit his wife and daughter to deal with any but the first dressmakers and milliners.

When a man goes hesitatingly in debt for twenty, fifty, or a hundred pounds, the purveyors of the goods

for which his flesh is weak enough
to crave, while his soul is not strong
enough to demand them authoritatively,
keep a wary eye upon him, and are
prompt with their little bills. But the
man who owes thousands at the best
shops in a place, and evidently does
not feel them to be the slightest
burden on his well carried and distinguished shoulders, is altogether
above suspicion and distrust. His
custom is considered highly creditable,
and he is, generally speaking, kindly
entreated and supplied regularly with
the best soles, while the mean-spirited
ones, who pay ready money, can only
get place and dabs.

Mrs Pottinger's late lamented husband had borne a bad name as far
as morals were concerned, but a re-

markably good one for the quality of his clothes, his horses, his dinners, his wines, his orchids and other stove plants. It was one of the modern miracles that he had kept himself going magnificently on the scantiest amount of cash conceivable. A vague idea, which had germinated in his own mind, that if several people died, with considerate opportuneness, he would come into a title, and large property had been transplanted into the minds of his creditors, where it had flourished and borne rich fruit for him. But now that he was dead, and had died disreputably, they, with one accord, swooped down upon the possessions he had accumulated, and brought forth bills that nearly broke John Treville's heart when his 'kind atten-

tion' was called to them peremptorily.

His sister and niece poured their
little private hoards of 'Bills Delivered'
in upon him also relentlessly, and
gave him to understand that they
would regard him as the typical
bloatedly, wealthly and brutally-grudging
relative of fiction unless he settled them
all and saved them further bother.

'Papa never let these things come
near us, he had such a fine chivalrous
nature; he couldn't endure the thought
of mamma being worried by sordid
money matters,' Alice, his niece, said
scornfully, when Mr Treville asked
how it was bills for such mere luxuries
had been allowed to accumulate in
this recklessly ruinous way.

'I can't expect anyone else to shield

me from the stormy winds of this cruel
world as my poor Fitzjames did,' the
widow wailed reproachfully. 'Still, I
did think, John, that brotherly feeling
would have softened your heart in this
terrible hour.'

It was in vain that John Treville
pointed out to her that even if brotherly
feeling reduced his heart to pulp, it
would not add one iota to his income,
nor keep the balance at his bankers
straight, if he acceded to all their
demands. They would not hear him,
but alternately cried, stormed, begged
and threatened until he felt mad
enough to sell Wingates, give everything into their clutches, and go bank-
rupt to get rid of them.

He only contemplated doing this
for a few minutes of temporary in-

sanity. Calm reflection quickly reassumed its sway over him, and he
knew that it was his duty to help
these helpless relatives of his to the
best of his ability, and knew also
that he would not fail in the performance of one jot or tittle of that duty.

But they were difficult people to help.

In the first place, when he mooted
the subject of the desirability of seeing about getting the landlord to
let them off the two years during
which the lease of their house had
to run, removing themselves and
the household gods that were their
own special property to Wingates,
and selling the remainder of the
goods and chattels by auction for the
benefit of the creditors, a stormy wind
arose that seemed to blast every poor,

secret, little hope he had half-uncon-
sciously permitted himself to nourish
about Rose Harlby.

'To go back to Wingates a lonely,
broken-down widow will be to consign
me to the grave a few months earlier,
that is all, John,' Mrs Pottinger told
him lachrymosely, while Alice sobbed
indignantly,—

'And to take me from Brighton and
bury me in that Cornish wilderness
will be to do me a cruel injustice,
uncle. What is my crime against you
that you should wish to rob me of
the chance of a home of my own
and happiness?'

'I left Wingates a radiantly happy
bride, in spite of poor papa's cruelty
to my dear Fitzjames,' Mrs Pottinger
cut in, before her brother could

answer his niece. 'To go back there, in my desolate condition, will be to reopen every wound which has been inflicted on me through life.'

'You would be mistress of the house, and as for you, Alice, if you have any reason left, you must know that your chances of gaining a good home and a husband, for that's what you mean, I suppose, would be greater at Wingates, where you would be regarded more as my niece than— than anything else—than they would be anywhere else. Where on earth do you want to go?'

'I want to stay here,' the girl said doggedly. 'I should die of dulness at Wingates. I hate country life and country society, for in this case the latter would be merely the middle-class people, who have run in one groove all their lives, and haven't an idea beyond the locality and their neighbours' business. Papa never could stand it, nor can I.'

'The bright air of this place, and the happy associations I have with it, are the only things that will keep me alive a little longer. Of course, if you feel the burden I shall be on you to be *too* hard and heavy a one for you to bear, you will force me to leave the home my dear Fitz. made for me. But I cannot think you have lost *all* feeling for your only sister, John.'

'And as for your being a burden on Uncle John, mamma, you are less likely to be a permanent burden on him if he lets us stay here, where I am sure to marry well and be able to provide for you, than if he drags us down to an out-of-the-way place that I've heard papa say is never trodden by the foot of any other man besides the butcher and baker, and a stray parson or apothecary.'

'Your father's foot trod it pretty often, worse luck,' John Treville was goaded into saying. Whereupon Mrs Pottinger cried hysterically, and his neice pronounced him to be 'a brute.'

After this outburst of feeling on either side, he felt it would be next to impossible to carry out his original intention and take the Pottingers home with him; and as soon as they knew he had renounced this intention they cheered up wonderfully, and then the responsibility of starting them afresh in Brighton came upon him with an airy affability, that made him feel at times as if he had been the pro-pounder of the plan.

His sister enveloped him in a sort of hazy confidence, in which he could not see his way a yard ahead of him without the aid and guidance of either herself or Alice. With a touching semblance of maternal pride and anxiety, she hinted vaguely to him that Alice and her admirable qualities had stirred the heart of 'one,' a most desirable 'one,' too, who had as yet been too diffident to speak out definitely, but of whom Mrs Pottinger was prepared to say with confidence that he was all she could wish, and would, she felt sure, do all that she wished.

'Do you mean that there's a fellow hanging about after her, who can marry and hasn't the pluck to ask her to marry him?' John Treville asked rather gruffly.

His heart was very sore about his own case, and he could ill tolerate the idea of any tomfoolery which might delay the removal of his obstructing niece from his own path.

'I am sure Mr Currie has every desire to bring matters to a climax,' Mrs Pottinger said stiffly.

'And I suppose Alice has the same desire, as she wants to stay here to be near him; it can't be she who is hanging back. What's the obstacle?'

'These delicate matters can scarcely be openly discussed, John.'

'Can't they. I don't agree with you there. The more openly they are discussed the better when the young people have once made up their minds that they care for one another; that is if the man means honestly.'

'He is everything I could wish,' Mrs Pottinger repeated stoutly, and her brother generously forbore to remind her that her judgment about men was hardly to be relied on since she was equally ready to declare that the late Major Pottinger had 'been all she could have wished.'

The end of it was that he yielded to their united wishes, and, after settling them in their new home, in a smaller house, but an equally fashionable part of Brighton (Alice stipulated for this, and Mrs Pottinger indefinitely gave him to understand that Mr Currie could not reasonably be expected to declare himself if they moved into the shade), John Treville went back to Wingates. Went back, perhaps, not a sadder, but unquestionably a considerably poorer man than when he left it.

He had deferred replying to Rose Harlby's letter day after day, hoping, against his judgment, that another turn of the tortuous coil of circumstances might enable him to respond as his heart dictated and hers desired. But day after day some deterring word or incident, or the development of some fresh awkward possibility prevented his doing this, consequently her letter still remained locked up and unanswered in his travelling-desk, when, on the evening of his return, Mr Harlby rode over to Wingates to see him.

In spite of his call being an entirely voluntary act, there was a shade of coolness in Mr Harlby's manner to John Treville. He (Harlby) knew that Rose's letter had been still unanswered when she left Gunwalloe Place a week ago. He knew also that Rose would have let him know at once if she had since heard from Mr Treville. Harlby's own happiness was mixed up with and dependent, in a measure, on Rose's fate. Accordingly, though he firmly believed in the perfect integrity of the man he had come to see, he felt rather aggrieved that the latter had evidently been unable to look at things from the Harlby point of view, rather than from that of the Pottingers' welfare.

They spoke of common - places, that were farthest from the minds of both for a time, avoiding the topics on

which each was in reality eager to con-
sult the other. At last Herbert Harlby
said,—

'Do you know that Miss Woodford has gone up to town with Mrs
Harlby?'

'No! has she? When did they?—I
mean, when did Miss Woodford get rid
of her New York friend?'

'When that lady's husband turned up
to take her back to New York, home
and duty,' Harlby laughed. 'Mrs Pollard waited for them to get clear away
from the sound of her barbed words,
and then gave a rather amusing, but
probably garbled, account of the husband's appearance on the scene at a
rehearsal of "My Queen of Love," and
the subsequent flight of the happy
pair. At my request, Rose went

at once to see Miss Woodford, and they have been together ever since. I thought you would probably have heard all this from Rose?'

'I have only heard once from Mrs Harlby; that was about a fortnight ago, while she was still at Gunwalloe.'

'God bless my soul, man! you don't tell me *that* letter closed the correspondence.'

'I am hampered, cruelly hampered, by my own family,' John Treville explained dejectedly. 'I have to pay down thousands that were owing by that scoun— by that unfortunate fellow, Pottinger; and now my sister and her daughter look upon me as a niggard and a tyrant, because I want them to come and live here quietly, instead of running me into fresh needless expense, by staying on at Brighton. I can't let Rose share my painfully encumbered lot.'

'You can, and you will, Treville,' Harlby said resolutely. 'When — after claiming my own, in a secret way, that savoured of guilt—I found that wretched brother of mine had left a wife and son, I swore to be a brother to her and to stand in a father's place to her boy. *You* know why the poor fellow who died had no legal claim to Gunwalloe. But, if chance had not taken me into that special carriage in that special train, I should never have known that I was the real heir. His blatant, bragging talk set me wondering and remembering, and, when I had the contents of his bag at my disposal, I knew that in taking the papers he had spoken of, I was merely taking my own property. But Rose

knows nothing of all this. The knowledge that he was a thief, as well as an
impostor, has been spared her. If she
ever does know it, she will think that
you broke with her, because you couldn't
stand the stigma that she will think at-
taches to her.'

' She can never know it — she can
never judge me so so wrongly, even
if she does know,' John Treville said
quickly.

' Frances knows the whole story.
I told her, though I have sworn
repeatedly that I would never tell a
human being, that my poor father's
illegitimate son had robbed his father
not only of money, but of every paper
that has been necessary to prove my
right to the Gunwalloe property. I
can't answer for Frances always being

discreet, if by chance any more whispering should be heard about me. My fair fame is dearer to her than anything, and exactly in proportion as she has misjudged me herself, is she now eager to let everyone know how bitterly she wronged me. If she tells Rose the truth about her husband's birth and his frauds—well, Rose will be lost to you altogether, and she will break her heart over what she will consider the disgrace. You had better put your pride in your pocket, old man? Come up to town with me to-morrow, and take possession and care of Rose, her child and her dollars, without farther delay.'

'I will,' said John Treville.

CHAPTER XI.

'Do you know, Herbert, I find it very hard to get rid of the feeling that I am a weak fool for loving a sinner, such as I believed you to be, all that time ?'

'I'm quite bad enough, dear. Be satisfied. You may go on nursing the delightful conviction that you're stooping in loving me.'

' " Stooping," indeed! I may nurse
the delightful conviction that I have
been a fool of fools not to have *felt*
all along that you were right—and my
absurd suspicions wrong.'

' My conduct gave a good deal of
colour to your suspicions. Only, some-
times I wondered, as you are a
shrewd girl, that it didn't occur to
you that the family lawyers would
have found me out in no time if I
hadn't been really my father's son, and
so the right man in the right place
at Gunwalloe.'

' Yes; there is something to be
said for me after all,' Frances admitted
candidly. ' But how can you excuse
yourself for having let me go on
blundering in the dark so long?'

' I wanted you to show me that

your love was stronger than your suspicions.'

'So it was. Didn't I go on loving you?'

'And didn't you go on suspecting me, too?'

'And didn't you go on tantalisingly giving my suspicions little dainty bits of food and sustenance. You should have remembered that I was only a woman, and have trusted me.'

'And you should have remembered that I was only a man, and have trusted *me*.'

'So I ought to have done, Herbert. Now, I know all about it. I feel that I was silly in the extreme for making such a point of knowing all about it. You were a hero all the time.'

'Indeed my conduct was unheroic from first to last,' he interrupted hastily. 'I walked in at the back door, when I ought to have walked in at the front, thinking that by so doing I was avoiding trampling on my father's memory.'

'You were lord of all you surveyed. You had a right to go in at any door you liked, and it was fine of you — you are a hero to have stood my taunts rather than betray your father's early peccadilloes. I know all that now, but as I didn't know it then, I want you to make me feel now that I was not so very much to blame after all?'

Naturally, he did his best to assure her in words that he held her perfectly blameless, and he endorsed his words by his actions. Still she craved for the liberty to make him fuller reparation.

'When may I tell Rose? She ought to know that it was my own desperately wicked heart and imagination that stood between you and me. She ought to know, too, that the attention and affection you have shown her, you have shown knowing her to be your brother's wife. I couldn't bear even for Rose to think it was anything else.'

He was only a man, not a hero, so this touch of jealously pleased him.

'You thought it meant something else yourself, I suppose?'

'Naturally, I did; and then, again, I wasn't to blame. That really was your fault, Herbert. How could I guess that the pretty woman who seemed to worship you was your brother's wife. You must admit that you played a dangerous game as far as she was concerned.'

'I don't admit it at all. I made no secret of my absolute devotion to you, and of my hopes of ultimately getting you to marry me. In the face of those statements a woman would have been a fool to fall in love with me, or to think I was falling in love with her, and Rose I knew was no fool.'

'Certainly not; all the same I should like to know, for a fact, that you were not the least little bit in the world in love, because you knew all the time that she was your brother's widow.'

Mr Harlby was silent.

'Come, Herbert; give me this additional happiness; say that I may tell Rose everything, and explain to her that your affection for her has been fraternal all along.'

'If she marries Treville you may tell her.'

'Why not if she doos not marry Treville?'

'Because—well, there was a time— it was a very brief time—when I ceased to think of her as my brother's widow, and only thought of her as a sweet, basely-used, lovely woman, whom it might be my privilege to protect from further buffettings from the world.'

'Then Herbert you were not *quite* faithful to me the whole time.'

'You had snubbed me and sent me off in a way that stung me, and on the top of your dismissal the discovery was sprung upon me that the man, whom I am ashamed to say was my father's son, had been an utter blackguard all through, even to the poor girl who believed herself to be his wife. He had a wife living when he married Rose. Mrs Gaston knew this, and that was the secret of her hold upon him.'

'And for the brief time you speak of you thought of marrying her yourself, and so making reparation to her for your illegitimate brother's sin?' She asked eagerly.

'My thought was not so definite as

that, dear,' he said tenderly, 'but I
pitied her so profoundly, that I felt
as if I could lay down my life for
her. You must remember that you
had cast me off utterly; and I am
only a man. Rose is as lovable as
she is lovely. Would it have been
very strange, if, thinking I had
altogether lost you, I should have
loved her a little?'

'Don't ask me riddles?' she laughed
rather faintly. Then she added much
more decidedly, 'What you have just
told me, proves to me conclusively
that it will be better, much better for
everyone of us, for Rose to know the
whole truth as soon as possible. While
she thinks that perhaps *you* might have
cared for her in the best way of all,
she will think of you as—well, as I

don't want any other woman than myself to think of you, Herbert.'

'The sooner you persuade her to marry John Treville, the sooner you may tell her the whole truth,' he assured her, and in return she gave him the promise that she would not leave a stone unturned to compass this good end.

'But he must do some wooing himself,' she said. 'Rose hasn't got over having had the advance she made in writing that letter repulsed by his silence yet.'

'Dear little Rose! How can any fellow repulse her?' Harlby said so earnestly, that Frances resolved to begin turning stones without any feeble delay.

.   .   .   .   .   .   ,

John Treville had gone up to town
as he had promised, but once there
his heart failed him, and his prudence
reassumed its sway. He could not
bring himself to do more than call on
Mrs Harlby, and tell her of all the
Pottinger difficulties which were be-
setting him. To these she listened
calmly and unsympathetically, he
thought, and the thought made him
denounce himself as a very unreasonable fellow for having anticipated
a show of warmer interest from her.

Instead of trying to develop this
interest, he took refuge from the
awkwardness of his misery by feigning
a great and absorbing anxiety con-
cerning the success of a new move-
ment he had just perfected, and was
about to patent, in a clipping-machine.

So he wasted the time in his first interview with her, and had to report 'no progress' to Herbert Harlby when they walked to their hotel together on leaving Rose's house.

He made no progress the next day, for Rose being informed by Mr Harlby that Treville was coming to call on her, went out and stayed away the whole day, and on her return home felt indignant with him for having missed her.

The next morning, however, his difficulties were dispersed in a very unexpected way.

He received the following, letter from his niece Alice :—

'DEAR UNCLE JOHN,—Nothing is so certain as the unexpected! We spoke of that lad young Currie to you when you were here. He introduced his uncle to us, the uncle from whom he had foolishly calculated on inheriting boundless wealth. People should never count their chickens before they are hatched?

'Mr Currie, the uncle, is a very superior man, very Scotch, and very much averse to being toadied by poor relations. I need not describe him though, as you will soon know him better. He made me an offer the second time he saw me, which I felt it my duty to accept. He has thirty thousand a year, and is going to make magnificent settlements on me, so we shall be quite independent again of you and everyone else, and after all there is nothing like independence!

The marriage will take place, by special licence, next Thursday. Mr Currie is no longer young, and says time is precious. If you like to continue to allow dear mamma a few hundreds a year I will not thwart your doing so.

'My future husband is Donald Currie, of Kilpankie Park, Kilpankie, N.B.— Your affectionate niece,

'ALICE POTTINGER.'

There was another letter from Mrs Pottinger, belauding herself and Alice and Mr Currie, and casually mentioning that the 'bridegroom elect was eighty-four' in rather a jubilant spirit. John Treville neither cavilled at the news, nor at the tone in which it was told, but blessed old Currie heartily, and went off with his news to Rose, who received it this time in a truly sympathetic spirit.

There was a double wedding very soon, but it is uncertain which bridegroom was the hero of the day, as uncertain, indeed, as it is which one is the hero of this story. But then this story was started on the lines 'No Hero,' and Frances and Rose are perfectly satisfied with the mere men they have married.

THE END.

COLSTON AND COMPANY, PRINTERS, EDINBURGH.

www.ingramcontent.com/pod-product-compliance
Lightning Source LLC
Chambersburg PA
CBHW032007060726
47497CB00017B/2367